VISIONS FROM THE HEART

RON BAESLER

DEDICATION
This book is dedicated
to the memory of
my brother
Larry Baesler
(1950-2007)
A farmer,
hunter and trapper
who loved and cherished
the outdoors, especially
western North Dakota.

(The cover is a picture of Larry
beside the Heart River)

"Time expands, then contracts, all in tune with the
stirrings of the heart."
— **Haruki Murakami, <u>Kafka on the Shore</u>**

"Have you also learned that secret from the river;
that there is no such thing as time?" That the river is
everywhere at the same time, at the source and at
the mouth, at the waterfall, at the ferry, at the
current, in the ocean and in the mountains,
everywhere and that the present only exists for it,
not the shadow of the past
nor the shadow of the future."
— **Hermann Hesse, <u>Siddhartha</u>**

<u>From the Journal of William Clark</u>
21t of October Sunday 1804.   a verry Cold
night   wind hard from the N. E…..   , at ¼ of a mile
passed the Mouth of Chess-che tar (or Heart
River)… 38 yards wide..i

<u>From the Journal of Meriwether Lewis</u>[*undated,
winter 1804—5*] 35 miles higher up, *Ches-che-tar_,*
or <u>heart river</u> falls in on the S. W. side; 38 yards
wide; not navigable except in high water, and then
but a short distance… in its course to the <u>Missouri</u> it
passes through open plains and meadows, generally
fertile, and always untimbered. there is some Ash,
Cottonwood, and Elm on its borders.ii

VISIONS FROM THE HEART
Part One: "Boldness and Breaking"

"I'm not afraid, no reason to be afraid." Every day during the first month of summer vacation he muttered this mantra to himself --as he gathered the eggs, carried out the table scraps for the hungry dogs, and as he walked down to the mail box to fetch the mail. If he'd been questioned, he'd have agreed with his mom, dad and most of the fifteen other children in the one room schoolhouse that had officially closed at the end of May. Of course, there was nothing to be afraid of. Going to town school was no big deal. In fact, it would be fun.

But at night, when he lay beside his sleeping brother in their basement bedroom, he stared into the dark and imagined the long, noisy bus ride into town. He could see himself crowding into a classroom with twenty-five sixth graders, most of whom had gone to school together for years. As he lay sleepless, staring into the chilly darkness, he told himself he wasn't exactly afraid. Anxious, maybe; worried a little. But not afraid. How could he be afraid with a name like Samson?

Samson...His mother had wanted biblical names for all her children. She was a religious woman with an earnest spirituality. Though he didn't yet realize it, Samson, her first born, had inherited that quality. His younger brother had received a biblical name too—John. Samson was devoted to his mother but secretly was irritated by her decision. *Of all the good, and even great bible names, why did she have to call me Samson? Not David or Daniel or Matthew, not Abraham or Samuel or Luke. No, she slapped Samson on me and I suppose I'll carry it to my grave.* Whenever he asked her why she'd chosen this name, she merely smiled and said she liked the ring of it.

In Sunday school, which he attended without fail, he'd learned that Samson, his biblical namesake, had encountered plenty of trouble with a woman named Delilah. Since he himself was not quite twelve, and didn't even know any girls his own age, he wasn't sure what kinds of trouble a woman could cause, though he supposed there were plenty.

The Bible's Samson was famous for his strength. The young farm boy imagined that the Bible's hero was even stronger than Charles Atlas, the muscle man featured on the back pages of the comic books he was allowed to read. This country boy knew that he was no muscle man. In his now shuttered country school, he'd been one of three fifth graders and he had no doubt that the other two could out power him.

One day, Betty, his classmate Donnie's little sister, bragged, "My brother can push a whole wheelbarrow full of cow manure out of the barn. Can you do that?"

Samson abruptly turned away and pretended he hadn't heard. The truth was, when it came to farm work of any sort, he was embarrassed. He'd never even dared try to move a wheelbarrow full of anything.

The Bible's Samson had a head full of long, luxuriously thick, black hair. Young Samson laughed when he thought of himself with long hair. No kid he knew, in country school or town school, had long hair. When you emerged from Eddie's Clip Joint, your hair was short. Eddie Gaugler, the high-schoolers called him Eddie the Butcher, was the only barber in town. He eyed every boy who stepped into his shop, welcomed him into his swivel chair, wrapped a sheet around his neck, and then asked, "So buddy, how you want your hair cut?" But no matter how you answered, he always administered the same haircut—bristly short—exactly what the parents expected from him.

So, even though he had no long hair, no great muscles, and no problems with females, he nonetheless carried the name of Samson, Samson Bartz, oldest child in the Bartz family. He'd not thought much about his name until this summer. In fact, he wondered if in his first eleven years he'd ever thought seriously about anything. Since the end of May, on the last day of class, when the teacher had announced that his sanctuary, his comfortable country school, was closing for good, his brain had been like the Heart River during the spring thaw, running, tumbling, surging nonstop. He'd been troubled and confused by this secret turmoil. *Are grownup minds always chattering along like mine has been doing?*

His young racing mind received an extra jolt when he heard his parents discussing how his summer would proceed. (According to his mother, discussing was significantly different from arguing, though Samson couldn't always discern the difference). His mom and dad were in the kitchen and Samson was reading, stretched out on the living room carpet, but could clearly hear their conversation.

"I think it's time for him to start driving the tractor, helping out with the field work."

His mother quickly replied, "No, no. I don't think so."

His father was quiet for a moment, perhaps taken aback by her abrupt and adamant response. "But the Krause boy is already driving their John Deere, and Henry Zimmer's kid is out on the field, and he's even a year younger than Samson."

Samson was surprised by the steel in his mother's voice. "I don't care about other families. He's too young, not strong enough. He's just...just not ready for that kind of life."

Samson held his breath waiting to hear his dad's rebuttal. But it never came. He heard his mother putting the supper dishes into the cupboard and the screen door slam as his father went outside. Samson conjectured that his mom had won this 'discussion' because she so rarely put her foot down. Maybe his dad was taken by surprise.

That decision shaped Samson's first month of summer vacation. His dad was up early as usual, milked the cows, had breakfast, then headed out to the hay fields. Samson had a few daily tasks. He gathered the eggs, fed the chickens and helped water the vegetable garden. Once those jobs were finished, the time was his own.

During previous summers, filling that time had never been difficult. Samson and his little brother would make up games, chase the cats, invent adventures. But now, on these beautiful June mornings, Samson would wake up, have breakfast, do his chores and then experience an unsettling disquiet. Just as we might have an itch in the middle of our back that we can't reach with either hand, Samson's mind prickled and squirmed. Even though the Dakota landscape stretched out endlessly in every direction and the azure sky went on forever, Samson often felt trapped.

One morning, late in June, he committed a blunder. He complained. "Mom, I'm bored."

She rolled her eyes, puffed up her cheeks and flapped her lips, "Bored? Go pull weeds in the garden if you're bored."

Her response was not surprising. But she failed to discern the changes her son was undergoing. Samson himself couldn't have described them. His unrest transcended boredom. Day after day trudged onward, steady and endless while his inner world craved... what? A surprise, a shock, something unique? He felt hemmed in. Until the day he found the skull.

*   *   *

Yes, this story involves a real human skull. But young Samson's discovery of it was neither terrifying nor amazing. His second encounter with the skull was not terrifying either, but it certainly was wondrous, and not only changed his summer, but impacted the rest of his life.

Late in June, on one of those days when Samson's mind was percolating non-stop and he'd grown weary of their simple games, he decided to go exploring.

Across the lawn from this home stood the Stone House. It had three-foot-thick walls made of prairie stones, covered inside and out with white plaster. The kitchen was centered around a coal burning cook stove. Shortly after his birth, a crank handle telephone had been installed on one of the walls. Samson had spent the first three years of his life in that house. But seven years ago, they'd moved into their new home and most of the Stone House rooms were now used for grain storage. One of the back rooms had an open stairway up to a narrow plank platform leading to a little door. The door was two feet wide and three feet high and opened into an attic.

Samson had long known about the attic and that door. He'd never felt compelled to see what was behind it. But this was one of those itchy days. The door became a magnet and he a shiny little nail. He had no trouble convincing little brother John to join him in an exploration adventure.

The first challenge was the open stairway. The two boys climbed cautiously, making sure their hands were always holding onto the dusty step above their feet. The catwalk at the top was only a couple of boards, barely two feet wide. They stayed on their hands and knees as they nervously edged their way to the diminutive door. A little block of wood nailed onto the wall held the door shut. Samson turned the block on its nail and the door silently swung out. The boys held their breath, but nothing stirred. The only sounds were the faint clucking of chickens in the yard below.

The boys crawled through the miniature door. By the light filtering through the dirty window on the east wall they could see that the floor of the attic was covered with a variety of objects, all layered in dust.

"Ooo..lookie Samson!" Samson turned to see John trying to put what looked like a green metal bowl onto his head.

"Johnnie, that's an army helmet." Samson snatched it and felt the dents in the metal. He imagined bullets whistling through the air. He murmured in awe, "I bet it belonged to Grandpa. He was in the war."

He lifted his eyes and saw a new marvel. He lowered the helmet and dropped to his knees. He barely managed to whisper, "Oh wow, wow." Leaning against the brick chimney in the middle of the attic was what appeared to be a giant bullet. The bronze casing did not sparkle in the dusty light, but to the two wonderstruck boys it gleamed like gold. Samson slowly extended his hand and touched its smooth side. Though it was cool under his fingers, he could imagine it hot, blasting forth from a battlefield cannon. He grabbed it with both hands and gazed down into its dark empty depths. He pictured his grandfather hunkering down in a trench with shells whining overhead.

Then, as he handed the casing to his brother, Samson saw it. He gasped, as most any boy would. But he was not terrified. He was, after all, a farm boy and he'd seen plenty of bones before, even skulls--at least animal skulls. But this definitely was not an animal skull. Tipped back on top of a sagging cardboard box, as if it were resting—was a very human skull, with very human teeth in a very human jaw.

Samson whispered in his church voice, "Dang, Johnnie, that's a skull, a human person skull." Little Johnnie's eyes were as big as eggs and just as white. Cold fingers of unease tickled the boys' necks, but the indifferent skull stared off into some far-off place. Samson's legs wouldn't move and his eyes were frozen on the smooth surface above the empty eyeholes. Now his stomach was icy and he decided he'd rather not disturb that skull or get any closer to those teeth.

He and his little brother backed out of the attic. Samson quickly closed the door and ensured the little block of wood was swiveled into place. The boys shimmied down the dusty stairs. For a moment their eyes ached as they stepped out into the glittery sunshine. To Samson it felt as though they'd returned from another world. They whooped as they ran to tell their mother what they'd discovered.

*　　　*　　　*

"So, you found the skull," their dad said. Naturally, their mom had told him the news when he came home from the field. Now, as he was chewing the last bites of supper he grinned. "Did you boys get scared?"

Samson glanced at his brother, then back at his dad, "Naw, we weren't scared, were we Johnnie?" Little John shook his head, though his eyes still had a frightened rabbit look.

Dad waved a finger at his boys, "You kids shouldn't be climbing around up there. That staircase and catwalk aren't all that sturdy."

Mom shook her head, "And you should have seen their clothes...totally covered with dust."

Samson was frustrated. Could they not see that this new land was more than danger and dust? He blurted out, "But

Dad, there's all kinds of great stuff up there. We found a helmet and a shell and—"

"Oh yeah, your grandpa brought those home from France. I wonder if Dad even remembers they're up there?"

Samson asked, "And the skull, Dad. What about the skull?"

His dad took another bite of peach kuchen before answering. "That skull's been around for years. Was my brother Raymond, your uncle who was killed in the war...he found it when he was a boy. It was sticking out of the Heart River bank after the spring flood. He saw something white, thought it was a rock. He dug in the soft mud and plop, out it came. Almost thirty years ago, I'd guess."

Samson persisted, "But, but...who does it belong to? I mean, who was it?"

Dad shook his head. "Nobody knows. No cemetery around here; no one found any other human bones. Who knows how long that skull was buried in that bank."

His dad reached for more kuchen and by the look on his face Samson guessed he was already thinking about all the hay bales he needed to haul tomorrow. But young Samson's mind was swirling. *Whose skin was once wrapped around that skull? Was it the skin of a an Indian? Or a dangerous runaway robber? Or a hairy fur trapper? Or....?*

"Samson, did you hear me?" His mother's voice sliced into his reverie. "Clean up your plate and take it to the sink. It's your night to do the dishes."

He soon was at the sink, washing and rinsing the supper dishes. In the soapy water, in the piles of suds, everywhere he looked, he saw that skull with its empty eyes staring off into some mysterious dark horizon.

*   *   *

How long could a restless almost twelve-year-old resist the lure of that attic and the siren call of that mysterious skull?

It was a Monday morning, the day after they'd celebrated brother John's eighth birthday. Even though Mom had protested that he was too young, John had gotten what he'd been begging for: his first bb gun. He was gleefully hunting sparrows out by the barn. Like every other mother in the county, Mom was doing the weekly laundry. Dad had left early on the tractor.

Samson's hand tingled as he opened the door of the storage room. The morning sun poured into the windows and every floating dust speck gleamed like gold. He took a deep breath as he climbed the staircase and crept across the platform to the miniature door. He swiveled the block of wood, the door swung open, and he crawled back into the dusty, dusky attic. His eyes were pulled to the corner where the skull lay. For a tiny second he imagined it was staring directly at him. He blinked and shook his head. *It has no eyes so how can it stare. Don't be a scaredy cat.*

Still kneeling, he walked over to the skull and warily placed his hand on its top. The bony surface was smoother and cooler than he expected. He sat down and rubbed the round bony bulb. *Inside of this there once was a brain that had thoughts and dreams.* Then he put both hands under the skull and picked it up. The jaw bone was loose. He was able to make the mouth open and close. Most of the teeth were still in their sockets. They were yellow, and to Samson, seemed larger than normal.

He sat down, set the skull in his lap, and looked into the skull's empty sockets. In the dusty half-darkness, the only sounds were the faint far away clucks of hens and chirps of birds. Samson was alone in this world. He leaned back against the chimney and stared into those endlessly black eyes, eyes that grew deeper and darker and larger until they swallowed him whole…..

*   *   *

Tachawin (Young Doe), the Lakota chief's winsome daughter looked up and smiled at Small Bear. He could feel his blood throbbing, his heart leapt—

His mother's sharp voice slashed into the teepee. "*Matociqala*, (Small Bear*)* it's morning. Go fetch water."

He groaned and pulled the buffalo robe over his head. For weeks he'd been aching to catch Young Doe's eye. For weeks, she'd deliberately ignored him. Now, at last, in this sweet morning dream she was approaching—

"Small Bear, you lazy good for nothing, get your bones out here now."

His moan became a growl as he threw off the robe. He pushed aside the skin flap and stepped out into the morning sunshine. His mother was holding out the deerskin pouch. Without a word he grabbed it and stalked down to the Heart River. He shivered as he dipped the bag into the dark icy water. Even though it was *Wipazutkan Wi*, the Moon of June berries, the mornings were chill on the northern plains and the water still held the memory of ice and snow.

He brought the dripping bag to the campsite. As he handed it to his mother, she shook her head and teased, "Fourteen summers old and you sleep more now than when you were ten. You really are a Small Bear, going back into hibernation."

He was a good Lakota boy; he loved and respected his mother. But she'd ripped him from his beautiful dream, reminded him of his youth, and called attention to the one thing he'd grown to detest, his own name. He grumped as he sat down and grabbed a piece of pemmican.

"Hibernation? I don't even know what that is. No bears out here on the prairie. I've never seen a bear. Such a stupid name…Small Bear. The other boys laugh when they say it." He chewed on the dried buffalo meat combined with tallow and chokecherries and tried to remember the smile on Young Doe's face.

"What are your plans for today?" Once again, his mother interrupted his reverie. When he only grunted in response, she teased. "You could come with me to pick berries. I hear that bears are very fond of berries."

"Huh, that's work for women and little boys," Small Bear muttered.

He felt a hand upon his head. "And this one certainly is no longer a little boy."

Small Bear tipped back his head and grinned. Grandfather's face was solemn, but his eyes danced with laughter.

The father of Small Bear's father was *Hanska Tahunta* (Tall Horse) He'd gotten his name many seasons ago, after a fierce battle when he'd led the tribe against the enemy, riding erect into a hail of arrows. Then he'd been an imposing, broad shouldered warrior. His muscles had been twisted ropes beneath his ruddy skin. His stature and bravery had won him the admiration of his people. No one doubted his courage. But beyond that, like one of the dark, ever-flowing springs that kept the Heart River cool all summer long, Tall Horse possessed a patient, endless wisdom. These qualities allowed him to be part of the *naca,* (the tribal council).

Now, he was over sixty, still lean and with head held high. Even now he was stronger than some braves, but his muscles had lost some of their bulk, and his once taut skin, now hung on him like an ill-fitting buffalo robe. Ten years ago, he'd been out with the men hunting buffalo. As they had thundered across the prairie, his horse stepped hock deep into a prairie dog hole. Both horse and rider broke their legs as they cartwheeled onto the hard earth. That winter was a season of slow healing and Tall Horse now walked with a limp.

Two years later, eight years ago now, his wife *Wichapi* (Star) died. Since then, his eyes, though still strong and full of sparkle, also held deep pools of sadness. Once he'd been the leader of the council—the final word in all decisions regarding hunting, battles, moving or staying. Now, he was still listened to and honored, still respected. But broken bones and a broken heart had hobbled his voice, and his spirit often wore a melancholy cloak.

Despite this loss of stature among the tribe, or more likely because of it, he had grown closer to his grandchildren, especially to Small Bear. He was one of those rare elders who had lived long and seen much, but still remembered the tumult of young boys trying to become men.

Tall Horse rested his hand on Small Bear's head and could feel the buzzing of the boy's irritated spirit. In mock seriousness, he commanded, "Stand up and let me look you over."

He laid his hand on the boy's shoulders and tilted his head to the left and then to the right. "Hmm, yes, definitely too old for berry picking. Maybe, possibly, old enough to join me at…oh, but I don't know…"

"What? What Grandfather? Join you in what? I'm old enough, I'm old enough." Even as he spoke, Small Bear realized how much he sounded like the little boy he claimed he wasn't. But the very thought of spending the day with his grandfather was so overwhelming, that like the current of the Heart River in the spring thaw, it swept away his feeble efforts to appear grown up.

Tall Horse's face tried but failed to suppress a grin, "I'm going to walk into the hills to the south, search for good arrowhead rocks. My cousin said he saw flint stones along the ridge. Too far for a little boy but maybe for a young man…"

Small Bear threw back his shoulders and scrambled to recover his manly composure. "Grandfather, I'd be honored if you'd allow me to join you in your search."

The old man playfully slapped his grandson's cheek. "Honored…. You just want to get out of berry picking. Come on, let's go before the day's heat bakes us."

The sky was silvery blue and a handful of clouds hung lazily in the sky, as though the fuzzy white balls from the cottonwood trees had floated up into the heights. The two figures walked through the dewy grass of the river valley toward the range of hills to the south.

Only months ago, Small Bear had needed to almost run to keep up with Tall Horse, but this morning he noted that either his own legs were getting longer or his grandfather's limp was slowing him down. The two walked easily together.

"When I came to your tent this morning, I heard dark words and I saw storm clouds on your face."

His grandfather had not asked a question, he rarely pushed, simply opened a space for his grandson to respond. Small Bear picked up a stick and swung it through the grass as they walked.

"Oh, I was complaining about my name. Doesn't fit. Doesn't fit me …'Small Bear'… doesn't fit this empty prairie."

Tall Horse walked along quietly until they came to the edge of the valley where the hills began. He stopped and turned and they both looked back to the camp.

The grandfather spoke softly, "Do you know who gave you your name?"

Small Bear shook his head.

"I did. Your own grandfather named you Small Bear."

The boy stiffened, "Oh, I didn't know, I'm sorry, I—"

Tall Horse touched the boy's arm, "No. It's all right. It's time you wrestled with who you are. Come, let's start climbing."

The meadowlarks' cheerful melodies escorted the two hikers up the low hills. Tall Horse moved steadily. His grandson kept pace but the youngster's mind was churning.

"Grandfather, why 'Small Bear'? Here on the plains, there are no bears. My name seems out of place, sometimes it makes me feel strange."

When they reached a rocky outcropping, Tall Horse sat down. "Let me tell you a story about names. Some names might seem strange but have a deeper meaning. Some names are meant to encourage. And some names are used to hurt."

Small Bear sat down beside his grandfather as he asked, "Names that hurt? How can names hurt?"

Tall Horse looked down at their camp, then let his eyes wander to the horizon. "We didn't always live on this unending prairie. When I was a baby, we lived near the lakes and in the forests to the east. Then from the north and the east, the Ojibwa people came. For a while we lived in peace. But then the trappers, the ones called the French came looking for pelts. The Ojibwe told the trappers that we were the enemies, they called us little snakes. In the Ojibwe language, the *natowessiwak*. To Frenchmen's ears, this sounded like *nadouessioux* and they shortened it to 'Sioux.' So they called us the 'Sioux', the snake people."

"But Grandfather, why would they do this?"

"Ah, Small Bear, it's easier to kill and harass people if you call them snakes. And that's what the Ojibwe did. Raids, then battles, many people died. When I was very young, we left the forests and came to the plains. Now we have our horses, our teepees, and the buffalo. They called us 'Sioux' to slander us, but we are the Lakota, the 'allies' and proud of our name."

Small Bear gazed down at the dozen teepees clustered along the Heart River as he silently chewed on his grandfather's words. During his fourteen years, his thoughts had never strayed far beyond the people of his own clan. Suddenly he realized that he belonged to a nation, he had a history. He spent a moment digesting this new reality but his youthful impatience soon intervened.

"But Grandfather, what about MY name?"

Tall Horse stood up and they continued their climb. He laughed, "Ah, yes, your name. When I was a small boy, I lived in the forest. In the spring, I often saw the bear cubs, lively, inquisitive creatures. They grew to be powerful, fearsome owners of the forest. So in the spring when you were born, I saw your dark hair and eyes—eyes that even as a baby were so alive. I whispered '*Matociqala*—Small Bear' and so you were."

They reached the crest of the hill and stopped to catch their breath.

Small Bear was warmed by the story, and yet, like a thistle, his frustration still pricked at him. "I know I should be proud of my name, but no one in the tribe understands, and out here there are no bears and…"

Tall Horse laid his hands on his grandson's shoulders and turned him away from the village in the opposite direction.

"Has no one ever told you about the holy mountain far to the south of here?"

"No…or maybe I wasn't listening."

Tall Horse chuckled and threw his arm across Small Bear's shoulder. "Ha, that is more likely." He raised his arm and pointed across the rolling plains to the horizon. "Four days ride from here lie the *Ȟe Sápa,* the Black Mountains. And standing as a sentry on their northern edge is *Mathó Pahá,* Bear Mountain. Bear Mountain is where the creator of the Lakota speaks to those who listen. Many young men have climbed this mountain on their vision quest. The mountain looks like a mighty bear, resting on its side. So, you see, Small Bear, your birth name connects you to what is holy among our people. One day I hope you'll visit this sacred place. Now, follow me."

Small Bear fell in behind Tall Horse as he walked along an animal trail that followed the ridgeline. The trail dipped and the old chief stepped off the trail toward a rock-strewn patch. He bent over and picked up a stone the size of his head. "Ah, here is what we've been looking for."

He held it out for Small Bear to see. One part of the rock was covered with a white crust and the rest was a smooth, dark blue that seemed to absorb the sunlight.

"Sit down and let's see what this flint rock will give us," Tall Horse said, as he opened the leather pouch he'd carried on his shoulder and withdrew a fist-sized stone. He sat down with the flint rock on the ground between his legs. He held up the stone. "This is the hammer stone. Watch now." He turned the flint rock several times, examining all its sides, then raised the hammer stone to shoulder level and struck the flint. A large shell-shaped chip broke off and lay on the ground. He picked it up, held it out for his grandson to see. Small Bear reached for it, but instead of giving him the chip, Tall Horse handed him the hammer stone. "Now you try it."

Small Bear reluctantly took the round stone. His mind was caught in a snare. He wanted to show his grandfather he was almost grown up, but at the same time he feared he'd end up blundering and demonstrating what a child he still was. He took the hammer stone and after a moment of hesitation gave the flint rock a cursory tap.

Tall Horse spoke firmly, "No, son. Bold, be bold. Strike with boldness."

Small Bear regripped the hammer stone, lifted it above his head and struck with all his force, once, twice, three times, until an irregular chip flew into the dust.

Tall Horse nodded, "Better, Small Bear, yes better. You have to be bold. Without boldness, we accomplish nothing. But now you need to add this: control. Look at the flint, see its character, its ridges and dips, choose your target. Then strike with boldness and with control. Now try again."

Encouraged by his grandfather's words, Small Bear inspected the flint rock. He chose a ridge on the flint's surface, raised his arm, took a deep breath and smacked the hammer stone down on its target. A piece of flint spun into the dust.

Tall Horse leaned over and picked it up. "A good strike, a usable piece. We might make this into a small arrowhead." He handed it to his grandson who turned it over in his hands, silently thanking the Spirit that he'd not totally failed in the eyes of this grandfather.

"Do you know how I got MY name?" Tall Horse's question broke into Small Bear's thoughts. For a moment the boy was taken aback by this question which seemed to have ridden in on some unknown breeze.

"Ah, sure, Grandfather, everyone knows the story of how you sat tall in the battle against the Pawnee."

The old chief took the hammer stone from Small Bear's hand. "Yes, I sat tall, I lifted my chest and stretched my neck as I sat upon my horse. But do you know why I was so bold on that day?"

Small Bear shook his head. He'd not heard this part of the story before.

"I was the lead rider of the war party. As we drew near to the enemy's camp, we entered tall grass, taller than our horses. The braves needed to see me, to see our direction of attack. So, I stretched up as high as I could go. My head was above the grass so I was visible to my people. Yes, I was bold, without boldness we accomplish nothing. But I wasn't foolish or reckless. I was controlled. Do you understand?"

Small Bear nodded. He wasn't completely sure he'd grasped all that his grandfather was trying to say, but he sensed that it went beyond flint rocks and naming.

Tall Horse held his grandson's eyes for a moment with his own intense gaze. Then he reached into his pouch and pulled out a six-inch piece of antler horn. "Very well. Now give me your flint rock."

The boy handed it to him and watched as his grandfather placed the three-inch piece of flint on a flat stone. Tall Horse knelt and placed the point of the antler down onto the flint. His grip tightened, his arm trembled and a flake broke away from the surface. He repeated the operation and another flake slid away. Again and again, he pressed and snapped away flakes.

Small Bear stared at the process with growing anxiety. His flint rock seemed to be in danger of disappearing. "Grandfather, isn't that too… I mean… isn't it going to break?"

Tall Horse sat back on his heels and held up the piece of flint. "Can you see what is happening? Every flake that I break off, makes the edge sharper. We can't make an arrowhead without breaking some of it away. The breaking is what makes it useful."

Small Bear expected his grandfather to return to his work on the flint. But instead, Tall Horse laid the partially made arrowhead down and with a small grunt, swung his legs out in front of him and crossed them. He tipped his head back for a long moment, then sighed and looked at his grandson with a half-smile.

"You're young, Small Bear, but not too young to hear this: Life is full of breaking. Maybe not yet for you… But someday… Breaking is part of living. When the breaking comes, we mustn't see it as our destruction, but as a sharpening, a way that the Great Spirit might make us more useful."

Small Bear watched as his grandfather's eyes filled with tears. He blinked as his own eyes welled, and a shadow of fear crept into his heart.

"But Grandfather, doesn't breaking hurt?"

"Oh, my son, it hurts. It always hurts." Tall Horse slowly nodded. "But if you stare too long at the hurt, it's like staring into the eyes of a rattlesnake. You become paralyzed, then struck and poisoned. No. When the breaking comes, you shoulder the pain, then hunt for how the breaking can make you more useful, help you become the brave man you must be."

Tall Horse's emotions and intensity began to overwhelm Small Bear. He fought to keep the sobs out of his voice. "I…I don't understand."

The old man stretched out his hand and placed it on his grandson's arm. "I know, you can't truly understand until you yourself… You remember when your grandmother died?"

Small Bear took a deep breath, "Yes, I remember I was twelve."

"When my Star walked on, I was truly broken, the wound was deep. She was the one who had rescued me from the darkness when I broke my leg. Then when she left, the hurt was so great…. I was no longer a husband; I was no longer a chief… I stared so long into the eyes of the snake. How could this breaking make me more useful? One day, I awoke as from a long, weary, gray dream. I awoke. And I saw you."

Small Bear's eyes grew large.

"Yes, I saw you, and your brothers and sisters and cousins. I saw the men and women of our village. And in your eyes, in their eyes, I saw my reflection: Grandfather, elder… an old man, broken and therefore, maybe, wise enough to listen and help."

Tall Horse fell silent. The ceaseless murmur of the plains wind and the faint cry of a high hunting hawk surrounded the two Lakota kinsmen. Then, Small Bear cocked his head.

"Did you hear that, Grandfather?"

The old man shook his head, "What? What did you hear?"

"It sounded like someone shouting."

Tall Horse grabbed the flint rock, antler and hammer stone as he scrambled to his feet. "Your ears are younger than mine. Let's go."

They returned to the trail and trotted along the crest until the village came into view.

"Look, grandfather. The teepees are coming down." Now they could both hear voices and see a flurry of activity. The tribe was dismantling their camp.

Tall Horse exclaimed, "The scouts rode out yesterday to the west. They must have found a buffalo herd. We'll be traveling by this afternoon."

The boy and his grandfather scrambled down the hillside and hastened across the valley floor toward what for months had been home. Small Bear eagerly threw himself into the activity. His grandfather's wise words were temporarily forgotten in the buzzing excitement of breaking camp. But he boldly strode up to Young Doe and offered to help tie up her deer hide bundle. And later that afternoon, as he rode with his family westward, he tried to imagine what life's breakings might feel like.

*   *   *

The sun was dying in the blood red western sky. Small Bear stood gazing up at the scaffold. His tears trickled freely onto his bare chest. The scaffold's four posts jutted ten feet into the twilight. The buffalo skin wrapped bundle lying atop the platform held the body of Tall Horse—brave warrior, chief, father and grandfather.

Three weeks earlier, the braves had brought the elder's body back to the camp. The buffalo hunt had been nearly over when it happened. A wounded bull whirled and gored Tall Horse's mount. The old chief had managed to jump clear as the horse fell, but the pain-incensed bull spun around and trampled the man before anyone could rescue him.

Now, the cuts on Small Bear's arms and legs were already covered with scabs. He, along with most of the adults in the village had gashed themselves in mourning. Like all of the men, he had hacked off his hair as a sign of grief for the elder chief, the grandfather who had now walked on. For three days after Tall Horse's death, no man ate and the lamentation among men and women alike was loud and constant.

Village life was slowly returning to its normal rhythm, though on many evenings, individuals would come to the scaffold that stood on a high bluff overlooking the Heart River. They would weep into the darkling sky and ponder the great mystery of *Wakan Tanka* (the spirit world).

Tonight, Small Bear's ponderings were not of the great mystery beyond but of the mystery Tall Horse had left for him. When his grandfather had spoken of a breaking, Small Bear had been puzzled. That bewilderment was swept away in a flash flood of grief when he saw his grandfather's lifeless body. His grandfather's words about breaking were no longer a mystery. But his perplexity ran deeper.

"What will I do with this ache?" He spoke into the sky, to the Great Spirit, to the spirit of Tall Horse. "How can this pain make me more useful? How can it bring any good to me or to anyone? Who will help me see my way?"

The boy-almost-a-man stood quiet and alone as the nighthawks dived and whooped after mosquitoes. The sky's colors slowly bled from blue to mauve to purple. When the stars began to glimmer, he turned and walked silently back to camp.

*　　　*　　　*

Small Bear was now fifteen. He straightened and stood pine-tree stiff. He stood at the base of Bear Mountain. The holy man had finished the prayers and ceremonies and had just given him the signal. He was ready to climb the trail leading to the peak, find the right spot and wait for the vision, the vision that would give him his adult name and shape his future.

A thunder storm had swept over them only an hour earlier. Rain drops glistened on the needles of the pine trees on the lower slopes. The late afternoon sun sketched a rainbow on the deep blue wall of cloud to the east. Before he began his climb, in order to honor a sacred memory, Small Bear turned toward the north. One year ago, two hundred miles away, on a bluff above the Heart River, his grandfather had been laid upon a crude scaffold.

At the very moment Small Bear began his climb, that scaffold, which had withstood wind, snow, and rain, slowly tilted toward the river. The buffalo robe, eaten by mice and insects, split as the scaffold fell. The bones of Tall Horse fell to the prairie and his skull, rolling to edge of the bluff, tumbled down the ocher sandstone into the silent waters of the Heart River.

*   *   *

Samson's ears woke up first. Drifting into his hearing, faint as though traveling from another time, came the sound of a rooster. Gradually the sound grew sharper and Samson recognized the arrogant squawking of their flock's harem leader. Once his ears had awakened, Samson's eyes soon followed. He lifted heavy eyelids and blinked once, twice before he could even begin to recognize his surroundings. Visions of the Heart River, Bear Mountain, the funeral scaffold, and thundering buffalo still flitted through his mind but they were like thinning clouds, wispy and dissolving like dreams. Soon he could look through them and see the dusky attic. By the light filtering through the dust coated window, he could tell it was still mid-morning. Slowly, he lowered his eyes. He stared at his hands, still holding the skull lying on his lap. For a sliver of a second he glimpsed the face of Tall Horse and a shiver run up his arms.

Samson carefully lifted the skull from his lap and gently laid it on the attic floor. He got to his knees and scuttled backward all the while staring at that bony face gazing cool and white into space.

He sat on his haunches and tried to comprehend what had happened. Climbing the stairs, opening the door, picking up the skull...all of that was clear. But then, the empty eyes, all he could recall was falling into the empty dark, dark eyes, followed by a dark, confusing swirl.

And then, then...before him, around him, within him, there had been a vivid, pulsing other reality; an experience, a vision so real he dared to believe he could still smell the horses and feel the deer hide of the teepee.

He gradually extended his legs, and shuffled to the attic door. As he descended the open staircase, he mulled over how he could explain this to his family. He'd slipped into another time. Within a space of minutes, an hour at most, he had heard and lived with another people, had traversed miles and years simply by sitting with that skull. Was it all a dream? A vision? How could he talk about his experience? By the time he'd reached the last step, he had decided. In that deciding, without realizing it, he took his first tiny step toward adulthood. He wouldn't even try to put into words what had happened in the attic. He would not tell his family nor his friends. No one would ever know. Small Bear and Tall Horse, their story and their lives, would be his secret. He closed the Stone House door and walked out into the clear morning sunshine.

Samson had been subtly altered. His parents, caught up as usual by the never-ending farm work, were too busy to notice. Or perhaps there was nothing visible to notice. Even young Samson would have had difficulty describing the alteration. But just as he still delighted in rolling his favorite root beer barrel candy around inside his mouth, Samson now rolled his secret story around his mind. It tumbled delightfully in his thoughts, and curiously, the story's presence eased some of the racing, anxiousness that had plagued his early summer days. It eventually influenced his behavior.

One night, a week after his encounter with the skull, Samson heard his father hang up the phone and grumble.

"Ernest can't come either. Everybody is hauling hay at the same time."

His mother said, "Well, I suppose I could drive—"

"No. I promised your dad I would never make you work in the fields. You've got the garden and the kids—"

Samson's mother responded with a rare edge to her voice, "You're not making me do anything, I'm offering to help drive the tractor so you can load bales."

There was a click in Samson's mind, just as when he put a disk into his Viewmaster and pushed down the lever. Suddenly this scene and his place in it came into focus. He stopped being a timid spectator and boldly announced, "Dad, I can drive that tractor tomorrow." He saw the surprise on his father's face and the beginnings of a protest from his mother, but he plunged ahead. "I know my legs are a little short but that field is flat so we won't need much braking and the clutch is on a lever and I'm strong enough to push it and pull it."

His parents exchanged a glance. His mother gave a tiny shrug of her shoulders and his father gave him a small grin. "Well, Samson, it's going be a hot day tomorrow. We've got a lot of bales to haul. If we start real early maybe we can clear that alfalfa field. Can you be up by six?"

He grinned back at his dad, "If you wake me, I'll be up."

*   *   *

A breathtakingly blue sky greeted Samson as he followed his father out of the house. He was careful to not let the screen door slam and wake his little brother. By six thirty he'd gotten dressed, finished his eggs and bacon, tugged on his battered baseball cap and was ready to work. He wore his gray sweatshirt against the morning chill, though the still air and the growing sunlight guaranteed that by afternoon he and his dad would be sweating.

He held up the hay rack hitch as his father backed up the tractor and when the tractor's tow bar reached the hitch's hole he dropped in the pin.

"Jump up here with me, Samson." His dad grinned. He didn't say anything more but Samson thought he could sense satisfaction simply in the way his father gripped the steering wheel and whistled into the morning air.

The quarter mile long alfalfa field was a half mile north of their farm yard. Hundreds of pale green bales lay in dozens of rows from one end to the other. They pulled up to the first bale and Samson's dad pulled the clutch lever and the tractor coasted to a stop. He got out of the seat.

"OK, Sammy, sit down and listen now." Samson sat down on the cracked plastic seat cover strapped around the metal seat. He put both hands on the black steering wheel. His back was straight, he did not fidget, but inside his heart was doing a tap dance as his dad spoke

"I've shifted into super low gear. You won't need to touch the gear shift stick. I've adjusted the accelerator, that's the lever right here. All you have to do is push the clutch lever forward until it clicks. The tractor will start moving and your job will be to steer from one bale to another. Got that?"

Samson nodded, then looked up into his dad's face to confirm, but his dad had already hopped off and was sticking his pitchfork into the first bale.

"Ok. Let's go." His father grunted and heaved the sixty-pound bale onto the hay rack and began walking forward to the next bale. Samson pushed the clutch lever forward with his right hand and the tractor began grinding its way ahead. He quickly returned both hands to the wheel and steered toward the next bale.

For the first twenty minutes, Samson was exhilarated. Inspired by his mysterious vision, he'd spoken up boldly and now he was doing real farm work, truly helping out his family. The toughest aspect of his task was turning the steering wheel in the soft dirt of the hay field, but since he only had to do that when they reached the end of the row and headed back, he had plenty of time to practice his whistling while they traveled from bale to bale. His dad's shout interrupted his reverie.

"Sammy, pull the clutch. Pull the clutch."

Samson yanked the clutch lever toward himself and the tractor halted. He swiveled his head and stared back toward his dad, afraid he'd done something wrong. But Dad was grinning.

"You got the easy job. I need a break." His dad's blue chambray shirt was already dark with sweat and his face glistened. Dad grabbed the red plastic water jug that sat on the platform behind Samson's feet and gulped down the icy water. He replaced the jug and climbed onto the hay wagon. The bed was covered with bales.

"I've got to stack these up. Otherwise I'll have to pitch every bale higher and higher." He began lining up the bales across the back, then putting a layer on top of them. When all of the bales had been stacked and half of the rack floor was once again open, he jumped down to the ground and looked up at Samson.

"Keep your eyes open so that next time, when the bed is full, you'll know when to stop. No daydreaming. And Sammy, when it's a long distance to the next bale, you can push in the accelerator a little too. OK?"

"Yes dad." Samson recognized that he'd paid less and less attention to his dad's work as the tractor had ground up and down the field. He chastised himself for losing concentration. He regripped the steering wheel, newly determined to not let his dad down.

An hour later, Samson pulled the clutch. The hay rack was full. Dad had stacked the bales five layers high from front to back. Dad jumped onto the tractor and reclaimed the steering wheel.

"Go climb onto the bales on the rack. Hold on when we go down the hill."

Samson scrambled onto the prickly bales and clutched their strings as his father shifted gears. He tipped back as his father opened up the accelerator and sped toward the hay fence. They stopped alongside a row of bales already on the ground. Soon his father was undoing the stack that he'd just made on the hay rack, tossing the bales onto the earth, then scrambling down and restacking them. This time the pyramid was fifteen layers high. Samson sat on the rack watching until his dad spoke.

"It would be a big help if you could push some of those bales to the edge of the rack so I wouldn't have to climb up and down."

"Sure, Dad, sorry. I can do that." Samson scrambled and did his best to drag bales to the edge. Once again, he was embarrassed. He'd sat and let his dad do all the work. As proud as he'd felt to be helping, he obviously hadn't yet grasped the concept of what it meant to be part of a team.

By noon, the sun was pouring golden heat straight down on their heads and they'd just finished unloading and stacking the second hay rack full of bales. Dad unhooked the rack and climbed up onto the tractor seat. Samson stood beside him. Alfalfa leaves and dust coated his dad's arms and he could smell the sweat that soaked his dad's shirt and trickled down his forehead.

"Hold on, Sammy."

Samson grabbed onto the fender as his dad shifted the tractor into high gear and they sped home for lunch. Even though he hadn't sweated like his father, Samson relished how the air rushing past them cooled his flushed face and neck. His mouth watered in anticipation of the lunch his mother had prepared.

*   *   *

It was six thirty in the evening when they pulled the last load of bales through the gate into the hay fence. Since this was summer in North Dakota, the sun would shine for two more hours. Samson sat atop the bales on the hay rack and quietly prayed that his father would not want to unload the rack before supper.

The afternoon had been an exhausting marathon. The morning's exhilaration had melted in the heat and dust of the afternoon's drudgery. As the hours dragged on, Samson simultaneously had admired his father's endurance and resented his inability to see how weary his eleven-year-old son was becoming. Samson's neck and arms were sunburned, he had a headache, and his hands had blisters from yanking the baling twine. His earlier pride in boldly offering to help was dissolving into a puddle of self-pity.

His dad killed the motor, then swiveled on the tractor seat and looked up at his son slouched on the top of the hay rack.

"Whaddya think, Sammy? Should we unload this last batch of bales?"

Samson desperately wanted to cry, 'I wanna go home,' but he bit his tongue and gave a weak shrug of his shoulders.

Dad grinned, "I bet your mother has supper ready for us, roast beef and mashed potatoes and fresh string beans. I bet these bales can wait until tomorrow, don't you think?"

Samson gave a relieved grin as he scrambled down from his perch, "I bet they can, Dad, and we don't want to keep Mom waiting."

*   *   *

It was nine o'clock and Samson lay exhausted in bed. He'd devoured his supper and graciously consumed his little brother's admiration and grinned at his father's commendation that he'd been a 'good farm hand.' He'd gone down to the chill darkness of his basement bedroom and climbed into bed completely drained, yet he could not reach sleep's release. John slept blissfully next to him but Samson's ears buzzed with tractor noise, his face and neck radiated heat and his hands ached. His mother had come downstairs and given him two aspirin and he now could hear her complaining to his father about pushing the boy too hard.

One part of him wanted to go upstairs and protest, tell his mom that the job had needed doing and he was glad to have been able to help. But in another corner of his mind, as he tossed and turned, a quieter voice pondered deeper thoughts. *Will I ever be as strong as my father? Do I want to be? Will I be a farmer like my father? Will I ever want to be?*

*   *   *

Samson stepped out of the school bus and paused on the sidewalk that curved toward the two-story red brick building that would be his educational home for the next six years. He moved aside as the rest of the excited passengers poured out of the bus. Squeals and shouts, hugs and hollers—the school yard was alive with friends reconnecting. Samson knew a few people in this new school but he was in no hurry to greet them. He was gathering his courage to step into this new world.

Though he wouldn't recognize it until later in his life, this past summer had been a watershed. On one side of the divide lay the soft, rolling plains of childhood full of easy, careless, carefree days. On the other side, lay a convoluted landscape--ravines full of questions, canyons where cravings and fears lurked, rivers surging with passions. At the divide lay the skull.

Throughout July and August, he'd had more days of working alongside his father. But there were days without field work, days when he would do small chores and then have hours of freedom. He and his brother invented games and adventures. But Samson also found times to be alone. He wandered along the Heart River that curved through the plain less than a mile to the south. As he tossed rocks into the lazy current and stared up at the tan sandstone cliffs on the far bank, he imagined where his uncle might have found the skull. Along the river, the remembered wisps of his vision always became more solid and vivid. In the dark waters he thought he could see Tall Horse's weathered face. In the rustling reeds he could hear his solemn words to Small Bear. Samson had chewed on those words all summer, considered how soon he would need to be bold, mulled over how September would be the breaking and the sharpening of his life.

"Hey Samson, Samson Bartz. Whatcha waiting for?"

Samson looked up the hill and saw Jerry Rowe, a town boy he'd first met in church a few years ago. Last year Samson had known every student in his little school, and every book in its little library. But that was a bygone life, a former world. Samson waved, smiled and stepped into his new world.

*   *   *

No one was asking the question, but Samson was convinced he now knew the answer. Aunts and uncles had asked him over the years, grandparents too: What do you want to be when you grow up? Over the years he'd given the typical little boy answers, gleaned from the shows he watched on the family's boxy TV: cowboy, explorer, detective. His relatives had smiled at his dreams.

But today, on a Tuesday morning at eleven, as he sat in Miss Jondrow's classroom, Samson felt an interior click, followed by a tiny twinge of satisfaction, much like the pleasure that came from placing the last piece in a jig saw puzzle. *I know what I will be when I grow up.*

The first three months in his new school had been as invigorating as a raft ride on a spring flooding river. It took only a few weeks for him to realize that his summer itchiness had been caused by his new self attempting to crack open an old cocoon. Breaking away from his comfortable country school and its tiny world had opened him up to new people, new challenges, new books and new ideas. Without that fracture, he never would have met Miss Jondrow.

This morning he and his twenty classmates were bent over their in-class writing assignment. Miss Jondrow taught music for the whole school and English for the sixth, seventh and eighth graders. Her cheekbones flared red and her eyes flashed fire if you didn't listen when she spoke. She was younger than any teacher Samson had ever had, and prettier. Sometimes as the class worked on hand out sheets she would walk up and down the aisles. When she stopped and bent to examine his work, Samson grew light-headed from her perfume and felt his face flush. He didn't yet know enough about himself to explain these feelings, though by the end of the year, with the help of his new buddies, he'd understand a bit more about love and lust.

But today, as he finished the writing assignment, what clicked in his mind had less to do with Miss Jondrow's appealing and powerful persona and more to do with the passionate way she'd begun the class period. She'd been sitting as they filed into class, tapping her pen on her desk and staring into space. When the bell rang, she stood.

"I'm sure all of you've been asked, 'what do you want to be when you grow up?' Trust me, some of you will wrestle with that question for a lifetime. Some of you think you already know, and maybe that's what you'll be: farmer, fireman, teacher, homemaker. You have that in your head and it could happen. Or maybe somewhere along the way, you'll stumble into something totally different." She'd wandered toward the back windows as she spoke. Now she returned to the front of the room. Her chin trembled and her eyes flashed.

"You know what this country needs? We need more storytellers, brave people who can use words to help us see beyond our own little world. We need writers to bring color into our black and white existence. Boxes, everyone wants to put us into boxes. Storytellers can tear open boxes, they can help all of us breathe and dream." She stopped quickly, as though embarrassed. She took a deep breath, "You could be a writer. Think about it."

Samson never learned what events or comments might have incited Miss Jondrow's impassioned plea. She left their conservative little town after that school year.

But her ardent words burned deep into his young heart. And from that day forward he was committed. He would become a writer.

VISIONS FROM THE HEART
Part Two: "Point of View"

His boys whooped, his daughter squealed and Samson breathed a sigh of relief. He killed the ignition and allowed the old Volvo to coast to a stop in the gravel in front of his parents' house.

The two scruffy farm dogs barked and circled the car. Their tails started wagging when the children emerged. It had been six months since the Minnesota Bartz family had been out to the Dakota homestead, but the dogs' noses hadn't forgotten.

"Grandma, we're here!" six-year old Lillian giggled as she ran into her Grandmother Helen's arms. Eleven-year-old Jeffrey and his eight-year-old brother Sammy were working the kinks out of their legs by running circles around the cavorting dogs.

Samson slowly eased out of the front seat and arched his back.

"Still having back problems?" Roland Bartz waited until his eldest son unkinked his back then shook Samson's hand.

"Hi, Dad. Yeah, some days the muscles get tight. And the seats in this old beater don't help any."

"So, why not get yourself a new one? University English professors must be getting big money, right?"

Roland laughed and Samson wryly chuckled at the double irony. They both knew university pay wasn't that grand; and conservative Roland had never in his life bought a new vehicle—car, truck, or tractor.

Samson scanned the farmyard where he'd spent his first eighteen years and then all of his summers home from college until his marriage seventeen summers ago. Grass now grew where the Stone House once stood. The new steel walled garage was surrounded by windbreak trees he and his brother Johnny had helped plant when they were grade schoolers. The trees now stood twenty-five feet tall, not a great feat by Minnesota standards but for the dry, harsh winters of western North Dakota, a testimony to their endurance. The Chinese elms next to the farmhouse, the ones he and his brother had climbed when they were boys, now were scrawny and arthritic, obviously near the end of their life span. Samson turned to get the suitcases out of the back of the station wagon. *Time...it wears out all of us sooner or later.*

"Son, so good you could make it," Helen squeezed his arm as he entered the house. "Left from Fargo this morning?"

"Yeah, Mom. We drove up from the Twin Cities on Tuesday, spent Tuesday and Wednesday night at the Holiday Inn and left about nine this morning. Diane's conference ends tomorrow noon and she's going to catch a ride to Bismarck and I'll run up and get her so she can spend a couple of days here too."

As they entered the house, his mother said, "The kids'll be downstairs and you can put your stuff in the guest bedroom." Helen paused then softly asked, "And how is Diane?"

The question fell like sand into the gears of Samson's mind. "Ah, OK, fine. Why do you ask?"

His mother made a small gesture with her hand. "Just asking, Son. Here, put your bags down in here."

Samson knew his mother's quiet demeanor belied a powerful intuition and emotional radar. Had she discerned the unease he had not yet managed to articulate to himself?

Two hours later, Lillian was helping her grandmother set the table for supper and the boys were downstairs with their grandfather washing up. The wall phone rang and since he was the closest, Samson lifted the receiver.

"Good evening, Bartz residence."

"Oh, ...it's you. Samson, hi, it's me, Diane." Samson could hear a tightness in her voice. He felt himself tensing. They didn't usually check up on each other.

"Yeah, it's me. Everything OK?"

"Fine, yeah, all good." She paused and after a few beats asked, "How'd the kids handle the drive?"

Samson's brow furrowed *We've done this drive dozens of time. Always been fine, even when they were younger.*

"They did OK. The usual squabbles." He paused and the static of the line filled his head. He thought he could hear his wife breathing but she remained silent. He finally asked, "What's up?"

"Ah, Samson, I've decided, ahh..I'm not going to come out to Bismarck tomorrow. I've got a ride back to the Cities." There was a pause and then a rush of words. "I've got lots to do. No. What I really...what I really mean...I, well I, I just need some time alone, some time away."

Samson pulled the phone cord around the corner, out of earshot of his mother. He swallowed before he quietly spoke, "Away? Like away from the kids, away from me?"

He thought he could hear tears in her voice, "Oh, Samson, please don't... Yes, yes, away. Just a few days, maybe... Tell the kids I love them." Then, 'click' and his ear was full of the hum of the empty line.

Samson slowly hung up the receiver. His mother, on her way to the table with her hands full of silverware, saw his cloudy face and stopped short.

"Who was it? What's wrong?"

Samson looked up, shook his head and tried to sweep away her concern with a wave of his hand. "Nothing's wrong, Mom. It was Diane. Just a change of plans. After her conference, she's heading back to the Cities."

Lillian looked up from her napkin folding. "But I thought Mommy was coming to the farm to be with us."

Samson could feel his mother's eyes on him as he answered his daughter. "She was, honey. But, well, she's got...she decided she has some work to catch up on."

His six-year-old logician wasn't satisfied, "Dad, it's summer time. There's no school. How can she counsel at the high school if there are no kids in classes?"

Samson was saved by his two sons thundering up the basement stairs and scrambling to grab their seats at the table. After his dad had taken his seat, they all said grace and filled their plates. The boys chattered about hunting and fishing and climbing into the hay loft. Samson felt no pressure to tell his sons about their mother's change of plans. Nothing could diminish their delight at being out here in the country. For them coming to the farm was always a great adventure.

In the writing classes he taught at the University, Samson often told his students to imagine themselves in an exotic setting and then describe their feelings. Now as he sat at the dining room table where he'd sat when he was growing up, he tried to remember if he'd ever felt the way his boys felt about this place. He tried to imagine their excitement. *I must have had wonder here too. Isn't that part of being a boy? But the memories lying like a blanket of fog over my time here are ones about escaping, breaking out of a cage...*

Helen was cutting slices of peach pie when John and his wife Susan walked in.

"Just in time for dessert," Helen smiled.

John gave his mother a hug. "I always have perfect timing when it comes to your pie."

He slapped his brother Samson's back, high-fived his nephews and tickled his niece under her chin. Then he paused, "Say, where's Diane?"

Samson tried to sound casual, "She's at a conference in Fargo until tomorrow and then is going to catch a ride back to the Cities." He saw the puzzled look on his dad's face and also caught the 'leave it alone' look his mother shot at her husband. John had already moved on to a discussion of how the wheat crop was looking and the extended weather forecast.

After a year away at college John had decided he missed the open spaces of Dakota and the challenges of farming. He'd returned to work alongside his father. Ten years ago, he'd married Susan, his high school sweetheart and rented a farmhouse two miles to the south of the Bartz farmstead. They'd wanted a family, but after a decade of trying, were resigned to being childless.

Susan's hand rested on John's arm as she regaled Lillian with stories of their new kittens. John had his arm around Susan's shoulders while he tempted the boys with tales of how great the fishing had been lately below the Heart River reservior.

Samson listened to their stories and watched their animated faces. *How do they do it? Ten years and they still seem so in love. Is it for real or is it just show?* Samson mentally scolded himself. *No, John has always been guileless. No fakery. Maybe not having children has kept them close...Or being together all the time on the farm...No...Susan works at the hospital five days a week... Seven years ago, how were Diane and I? Were we ever as close as they seem to be? How do they do it?*

"Anyone for seconds on pie?" Helen asked as she rose from the table.

"I'll take some, Grandma," Jeffrey said as he held up his plate.

"That's what I like to hear. You must be growin'. Go for it." John gave the boy a high five. He and Susan stood, "We've got get moving. But I tell you what, if it rains tonight and we can't do any haying tomorrow, then I'll take you all fishing." The three children whooped as the couple headed out the door.

The dogs barked as the car left the yard. Helen smiled, "That couple, they always keep things hopping."

Samson nodded, "Johnny's always been a live wire. But if it doesn't rain tonight, I'm gonna have some disappointed kids to deal with."

Roland grunted as he rose from the table, "Oh, son, you worry too much. Always have. One way or another they'll be fine."

*   *   *

Samson stepped out into the cool night. One thing he did miss living in the humid, summer time stuffiness of Minneapolis was the Dakota nights. Out here on the western plains, no matter how baking hot the day might be, the nights always offered a chilly reprieve.

It was ten thirty and the sable sky was sprinkled with pinpricks of light. The Milky Way, invisible in their urban Minneapolis home, out here was a bold white streak directly overhead. Samson walked away from the house and out past the barn. He stood in the pasture, lifted and extended his arms and slowly spun in a complete circle.

It's easy to see why the ancients thought the sky was a round bowl full of holes back lit by the light of the gods. But what we think we see is not always what is. These stars might not even exist anymore. Their light has taken a billion years to reach my eye. Who knows if they're not already dead? And everything moves. The earth spins, it races around a sun that dashes through a galaxy, and the galaxy does a cartwheel dance through endless space.

And what about us, Diane? What about you and me? Are we still what we think we are? What direction have we been moving these last seventeen years?

*   *   *

The next morning, his son Sammy's delighted squeal dragged Samson from his fitful slumber. He lay on his back in his parents' guest bedroom with his eyes closed. Last night, after an hour of tossing and turning he'd finally managed to sleep, only to be awakened by the rumbling, windy passage of a thunderstorm. He'd fallen back to sleep to the sound of rain, comforted knowing that his children would have their fishing trip in the morning.

Now Samson could hear his ecstatic son celebrating that good news. He opened his eyes, rolled out of bed and groaned as he tried to straighten his back.

"Ohh. Damn muscles. Gotta keep doing my back stretchers," he muttered as he pulled on his cut-offs. Six months ago, he'd gone to see an orthopedist about his lower back pains. He described his symptoms and the first thing the doctor said was, "Do you have any issues causing stress in your life?"

The question obviously unnerved Samson and the doctor smiled, "You weren't expecting that from an orthopedist, I'll bet. But lower back tightness is often related to tensions caused by unresolved emotional situations. Anything going on with you?"

Samson wasn't about to be psychoanalyzed by someone he'd just met. But he didn't need to delve too deeply into his more personal struggles.

"I'm two months into a new teaching position at the U of M. Four months ago, we moved from Winona, bought a house, got the kids enrolled in new schools." He gave the doctor a wry grin, "Are those enough stressors for you?"

The orthopedist had nodded, ordered a CAT scan and then sent him to a physical therapist. After five treatments, the therapist gave him a series of back stretching exercises. The exercises helped, but he had to do them every day in order to keep the muscles loose. The tensions that kept triggering the muscle cramping in the first place—Samson hadn't found a way to diminish those.

He shuffled out of the bedroom to the kitchen and poured himself a cup of coffee.

"Daddy, we're going fishing. Uncle John is going to take us all fishing." Sammy hopped and twirled around his father.

"That's great. I'm sure you'll catch a big walleye."

"What about you Daddy? What do you want to catch?"

"Me? Ahh, I think I'll catch up on my work and my sleep."

Samson's mother looked up from where she stood over the pan of sizzling bacon. "You mean you're not going with us?"

"Nah. You know me Mom. Fishing has never been my thing. Johnny's the big fisherman and I know Dad likes to be out. I'll let you all go out. The kids'll love it. I've got to get a syllabus ready for the fall...and maybe I'll take a nap."

"So...you didn't sleep well? The mattress is new," she shrugged as she cracked eggs into the hot pan.

Samson sat down at the table. *Is she sensing something with her radar? Or are my nerves overreacting?*

Breakfast was raucous. Grandpa Roland's teasing was an expression of love and he was delightedly baiting his grandsons.

"I'll bet Lillian catches the biggest fish today. You boys are too squirrely to sit and watch your bobbers."

"Oh yeah, I'll bet you a dollar, Grandpa, that my fish will be bigger," Sammy grinned.

Roland leaned toward his exuberant grandson. "Do you have a dollar to bet?"

Sammy spun in his chair, "Daddy, can you give me a dollar?"

Samson joined the laughter around the table. "When you come back home, I'll measure your catch and then we'll settle all bets."

Roland grabbed another piece of bacon and said to his son, "I hear you're skipping out on the fishing. Your loss. But if you don't mind, while we're gone, could clean up the old grill? We'll have a mess of fish to cook up for supper, won't we, kids?"

The blare of John's pickup horn catapulted the kids out of their chairs. Helen grabbed the picnic basket and Roland went out to the garage to gather up the rods and reels. Samson stood on the porch with his coffee mug and waved them on their way.

After the dogs returned from noisily escorting the pickup out of the yard, the hushed blanket of the Dakota morning enveloped Samson. No chickens cackled; his parents had stopped raising them. No cattle bellowed; they were all grazing in distant pastures. Even the usual Dakota breeze was dormant. The silence, so much a part of life in this country, so much of what he'd grown up with, now was unnerving. It accentuated the unrelenting clamor within his mind.

Haven't I always taken care of Diane and the kids? Made sure the bills were paid, insurance up to date. Haven't all our moves been made to better our lives, their lives?

He took his coffee cup back into the kitchen and noted the dirty dishes in the sink. When he was growing up, his mother could never leave the house until the dishes were washed. Evidently she'd managed to free herself from that compulsion.

But still, how little Mom and Dad have changed. Same house, same church, same friends.The changes Diane and I have endured in the last seventeen years…so many times we've moved…so many different chapters we've written.

Samson decided to wash up the dishes and, with his hands in the soapy water, he mentally paged through their story.

He and Diane had married weeks after their college graduation. Diane had applied for a job as a community outreach worker for the local food bank. On the day she was scheduled to come in for an interview, Samson received word that he'd been accepted into the graduate program of the English Department at the University of Minnesota. Diane skipped the interview and began gathering their few possessions. They packed their worldly belongings in a small U Haul trailer and moved into a tiny apartment near the Minneapolis campus.

From the first day Samson was swept into the maelstrom of reading and writing required by his doctoral program. Diane discovered that jobs for new social work graduates were limited and fiercely contested. For a year she worked as a restaurant hostess, then during Samson's second year she found work as a manager of a small bakery. In year three Samson's thesis proposal was accepted and Diane finally found work in her field. She was hired as a behavioral management aide in a local junior high. During the fourth year of graduate work, all of Samson's days and many of his nights were spent researching, reading, formulating arguments and writing the chapters of his thesis. Diane, searching for ways to fill evenings and weekends, found community in a local church where she sang in the choir and participated in a women's group.

In the spring of 1975, Samson successfully defended his thesis: "Time Travel as a Plot Device in Science Fiction and Fantasy Literature." He proudly marched across the stage to receive his doctoral stole, to the applause of Diane and his parents. The next month was momentous. Samson accepted a teaching position at the junior college in Janesville, Wisconsin and Diane became pregnant. She received the congratulations from her church family and her colleagues while at the same time tearfully bidding them farewell.

Samson thought of this as 'Chapter One' of their marriage. Chapter Two would probably be called 'Teacher and Two Boys.' He began his career as a teacher and four months later son Jeffrey was born. Thirty-six months later son Sammy entered the family. This was a short chapter, only three and a half years.

Chapter Three began with an invitation to an assistant professorship position at Winona State. Samson thought

'Climbing the Ladder' might be a good name for that chapter. During his seven years there, he published a book of short stories and was promoted to associate professor. Lillian was born one year after their arrival.

Chapter Four began one year ago. Winona had been their home for seven years when Samson was offered his dream job: a tenure track position at his alma mater, the University of Minnesota. Though they had a beautiful home, the boys loved their school, and Diane had begun training in a counseling program, it was decided that this was an opportunity Samson could not turn down.

In May he finished his first year of teaching and now imagined himself solidifying his career at the U.

Samson had washed and dried the dishes and was putting them in the cupboard when a question struck him. *What titles would Diane give to the chapters of our life? How would she describe our story?*

He stepped back out onto the porch into a morning that was becoming stuffy and hot. *She always supported me. All our moves, we always discussed them together. She never complains. She's never protested. She's such a great mother.*

Samson remembered his dad's request and headed out to the garage. He found a steel wire brush on his dad's workbench, then returned to the back yard. He opened up the old grill standing next to the house. The grates were crusted with black, burned-on grease.

Jeez, Dad, when's the last time you cleaned this beast.

He began scraping. At the bottom of the grill, beneath the grates lay a few charcoal briquettes edged in white ash. The sight triggered a memory from three months ago. He'd been reading the Saturday Minneapolis Tribune.

"Hey Diane, listen to this."

Diane was sitting at the kitchen table, writing up a grocery shopping list.

"There's an article here about this lignite field twenty miles out of Medora, in the Badlands. You know, just 50 miles from the old farmstead."

She did not look up from her writing, "I know where the Badlands are."

Samson read from the paper. "Last week, two hikers left a Badlands hiking trail and wandered among the buttes. They wandered into a valley and were struck by how warm the air had suddenly become. Then they noted that the ground beneath them was extremely hot and heard a rushing noise. They moved slowly forward. Then suddenly, a mere fifteen feet in front of them, the ground slumped as smoke and ash shot into the air. Park rangers determined that the hikers had stumbled onto an underground coal vein that had been burning and smoldering for years and had finally reached the surface."

Samson looked up. "Those kids were lucky. Just imagine that scene—a bland, peaceful, innocent looking prairie, but hiding underneath, is a seething, smoldering inferno."

Diane finished her list and stood, "Reminds me of some of the high school boys I've been counseling." She headed for the door and just as she left the room she muttered, "And of some marriages I know."

Now, months later, as Samson scraped greasy crust from the old grille, he remembered being puzzled and vaguely anxious by Diane's words. He had even planned to ask her whose marriages she had in mind. But he'd spent the morning golfing with new colleagues and then taken the boys to soccer practice in the afternoon. By the time dinner was over and bedtime stories had been read to the three children, her words and his feelings about them had drifted downstream and out of his consciousness.

But now, as he scoured the filthy grates and a sheen of sweat appeared on his forehead, Diane's throw-away comment of three months ago echoed ominously in his mind.

Is she angry? Furious? Fuming? How can that be? We don't fight. Our arguments are so few and so trivial. Have I been oblivious? What am I missing?

He got a battered old bucket from the garage, tipped the grill sideways and scraped out the detritus. He set the grill back upright and carried the bucket out into the tree stand. As he scattered the waste onto the dirt, a pin prick of fear stabbed his mind.

What if, ...what if Diane has been harboring this, this...resentment for years? Hiding her frustration and fury under her calm competence? Might I be heedlessly walking on dangerous ground?

I've spent hours and hours teaching students how to read stories, analyze plots, discern revealing details and discover an author's intentions. Have I been so unmindful of the story we've been living together?

Despite the sultry midday air, a shiver ran down his back. How would he cope with any jagged holes in the carefully constructed life narrative he'd mentally been composing since his college days?

He returned to the garage and tried to shove the bucket under the work bench. An old faded cardboard box stymied his effort. He bent over and pulled it out. After he pushed the bucket back under the counter, he opened the flaps of the box and there it was: the skull.

He sat back on his haunches and gazed at the bony crown. *I can't believe Dad has still hung on to this. But then, what else could he do with it?*

Samson picked up the box, stood and walked to the backyard. He set the box on the picnic table and went into the kitchen. A few minutes later he emerged with a beer. He grabbed the weathered aluminum-framed chaise lounge lawn chair and pulled it up alongside the table. He set down his beer and carefully lifted the skull out of the box and set it on the picnic table's bench. Then he grabbed his beer and cautiously lowered himself into the lawn chair, hoping the frayed plastic bands were still strong enough to hold his weight.

He sipped his beer and stared at the skull. The jaw bone was still intact. Most of the teeth were still in place.

He was swept away by a torrent of images, memories and emotions. He was transported a quarter century into his past. Before his resolve to escape the farm, before his commitment to become a writer, before...when he was still a boy...He remembered that summer day when he and John had climbed the Stone House stairway into the attic and come face to face with this bony grin.

*Ahh, yes. Then we were wonder struck. Little boys staring
at the skull of an unknown man. We held our breath, we
whispered and slid on our knees backwards out of that attic.*

Scenes from that summer now floated through Samson's
mind, swatches of memory: working for the first time
alongside his father, lying sleepless in bed desperately
seeking to quell unformed fears, walking for hours alongside
the Heart River's dark waters.

He held the beer bottle against his cheek. The glass cooled
his face, but his broodings grew more agitated. His mind's
probing fingers stretched toward a light, an image, a world
but they grasped only vaporous clouds.

*Something more, I'm sure there was something more.
Didn't I see this skull once more? Didn't something, someone
appear?*

The more Samson's thoughts probed his past, the less sure
he was of his intuition. And yet, one fragile, fleeting vision
kept dancing on the edge of his consciousness: dark eyes in
a weary face, and a warm voice...a man's voice, rich with
tears.

He set the bottle on the table beside him and picked up the
skull. He set it onto his lap. He stared into those endlessly
black eyes, eyes that grew deeper and darker and larger until
they swallowed him whole.

*   *   *

John plunged his face into the water and opened his eyes. The late
afternoon sunlight pierced only two feet into the murk. He surfaced, flinging
jeweled droplets of water into the air from his long black hair. "Can't see a
damn thing."

His partner Peter, standing on the river bank above him, laughed. "What
did ya expect? This ain't no mountain stream. It's the Big Muddy. Walk out a
ways, feel with your feet. That sack can't be more than a five, six feet away
from shore."

The two men had spent a long day poling and paddling their canoe against
the slow but relentless current of the Missouri River. Seven years earlier,
when the two men had been part of the thirty-three-man crew assembled by
Meriwether Lewis and William Clark, the boats had been bigger and the man
power plentiful. But now the only muscles belonged to thirty-year-old Peter
Weiser and twenty-eight-year-old John Thompson.

They had decided to quit for the day and had been unloading the canoe so they could pull it out of the river when the canvas bag containing their pots and pans splashed into the murky water. Now they were trying to retrieve it.

John sighed, gulped his lungs full of air and plunged back down. He surfaced, shaking his head like a wet dog. "I got it. Help me up."

Peter grabbed John's outstretched arm and helped him up the slippery bank. They finished unloading their canoe and set up camp. They'd chosen a grassy clearing surrounded by hackberry trees on a rise ten feet above the mile-wide river. They had a small amount of dried meat in their supplies but intended to reserve it if at all possible. The sun was setting and the flies were hovering above the glassy river. John walked a hundred yards downstream and after only ten minutes of casting his fishing line, managed to land a six-pound northern pike. After scaling and gutting it, they roasted it in a small fire fed with sticks from fallen branches.

The August evening was warm and the combination of smoke from their fire and a gentle westerly breeze, kept most of the mosquitoes at bay. John, sitting on the grass, stretched out his legs and leaned his shoulders against a fallen cottonwood trunk. "How far you reckon till the mouth of the Heart?"

Peter swirled the last of his coffee in his tin mug. "You're the one who's done surveying. Today as we paddled, didn't you recognize any landmarks that we passed with the expedition?"

"Hell, that seems like a lifetime ago. Besides, if I remember rightly, about that time we were too worried about Indian attacks to notice landmarks."

Peter nodded, "Yeah, guess so. Who'd have guessed we'd end up spending the whole damn winter surrounded by those savages."

Like everyone on that expedition, John too had called all the native peoples they'd met on that trek 'savages'. But now, as he gazed into the ruddy embers of the dying fire and remembered the faces of the men, and the faces, and especially the bodies, of some of the women from the Mandan tribe, he mentally recoiled from that term. The natives he'd come to know were neither brutal nor primitive. Yet, John hesitated to speak. Peter was the leader of this new enterprise. Peter had called him 'partner' but John believed himself to be a junior member of the team and was convinced Peter saw him that way too. Rather than challenge Peter, he decided to change the conversation.

"That was a long winter. Wasn't all bad though. The first few months going upriver we all worked our asses off but were too exhausted to get to know the other men. Those long winter months in the fort…by the time spring came, we were all friends."

Peter snorted, "Naw, not all of us. Some of those assholes were never my friends."

John back-pedaled reluctantly, "Alright, maybe not friends, but at least we all knew each other better, we came out of that winter a stronger crew."

Peter tossed the dregs from his cup into the flickering embers of the fire. "Maybe so, but I still say we'd a been better off if some of 'em had stayed at Fort Mandan."

An hour later the two travelers lay under their blankets on the soft grass. Peter had declared that because the night was warm, they would not set up their tent. His soft snoring now harmonized with the chirping of the crickets and the occasional croaking of the bullfrogs. As John drifted toward sleep, a thought, like a stick floating on the river, kept bobbing to the surface. *We've travelled the same waters, come face to face with the same people, and yet it seems our eyes have seen different worlds. Will our worlds ever come together?*

*   *   *

By eight am the next morning the men had been on the river for two hours. Tall cottonwoods lined both banks. The sun had already burned off the river mist and was now heating up the moist air. John, paddling from the front of the canoe, was squinting into the glare, scanning both banks for clearings and the earthen mounds that housed the members of the Mandan tribe.

Abruptly, Peter pulled his oar from the water and shouted, "Hold up John, I think we've arrived." Ahead, just where the broad Missouri curved northeastward, a small river, a hundred yards wide, sliced in from the northwest. Peter pulled a small map from a leather pouch around his neck.

"According to Clark's map this is the Heart River. We were here on this spot, on October 18, 1804, a little less than seven years ago. Yes siree, this is it."

To John the river looked insignificant but he tried to match his partner's enthusiasm. "So, this is where we start making our fortune."

As soon as they paddled into the mouth of the tributary, the current dwindled and then disappeared.

"No mountain snows feeding this river," muttered Peter as they slid their canoe onto a sandbar a hundred yards farther upriver. They climbed up the bank and surveyed the Heart as it coiled northeastward through low hills. John wondered how long he'd have to wait before Peter began expounding on The Plan.

John had been hearing versions of The Plan for weeks as they'd moved up the Missouri. The first time he'd heard it was six months ago in a dim, dirt-floored bar in St. Louis.

Like many of the men in the Lewis and Clark Expedition, John's perspective had been altered by his twenty-eight month, eight-thousand-mile round trip journey to the Pacific Ocean. Most of the nation's citizenry knew that to the west lay 'wilderness'. But John, Peter and the others had traversed the endless plains, summited the peaks, forded the whitewater rivers and stood on the shores of the great ocean. For all these men, 'wilderness' was now a vibrant reality. For some of them, like John, that wilderness now made their family's orderly farms and bounded orchards feel like confining stockades.

John had spent a few years working with his brothers on the family farm, then done some surveying work in the western part of Indiana. But he could not shake off the urge to move, to travel. Two years ago, he'd hired on to help move flatboats laden with flour down the Ohio River to the Mississippi and on to New Orleans. On a chill evening this past March, he stepped into a bar a hundred yards from the docks in St. Louis. Before he even ordered a beer, he heard the first version of The Plan.

A man sat at a low table with his back to John and was holding forth to a half dozen grizzled men, "The Frenchies told us that some of those short rivers had never seen any trappers. Some of 'em, like the Heart River are full of side streams and coulees, perfect spots for mink, weasel, muskrat, and of course, beaver, lots of beaver."

At the mention of the Heart River, John snapped to attention and as he moved closer the voice grew familiar.

"I plan on finding a partner, traveling up the Missouri and trapping out that river. The Frenchmen come down every winter from Canada to deal with the Mandan and Hidatsa. We'd sell our furs to them, wouldn't need to bring down river. After the Heart, hell, there's the Little Missouri, the Yellowstone, the land is teeming with furs."

John heard the names of those rivers and his heart expanded and he could see again the vast sky and hear the thundering of the buffalo. He moved to the table and grinned down at the assertive speaker, "Peter Weiser, what are you doing here in St. Louis, other than filling men with wild ideas?"

Peter looked up, a small grin on his face. He stood because he recognized a fellow Expedition member. But by the squint of his eye, and a second of hesitation, John could see that Peter couldn't remember his name.

He extended his hand, "John, John Thompson, Indiana, helped a little with the map making on the way upriver."

Peter nodded, smiled and pumped John's hand, "John, of course, of course. I remember. What are you doing in these parts?"

John brought his beer to the table. The other men slowly drifted away as Peter and John swapped stories of how they'd tried unsuccessfully to settle down into their old lives. The hours passed and by the end of the night, Peter had spoken so compellingly of The Plan that he'd convinced John to be the partner that would help him execute it.

Now, six months later, the two men stood on the bluff above that river. The buffalo grass was only ankle high, already baked brown and stiff from the summer heat. Both men knew that after the heat would come the cold, the biting chill that not only caused the animal furs to grow long and lustrous, but threatened the lives of those who tried to trap those animals.

"First off, we gotta decide where to build our shelter," Peter announced. "Doesn't have to be fancy, but we need to keep out the wind and at least some of that damn cold."

John ventured, "Maybe we could do like the Mandans, make a small earth lodge. Those seemed good protection against the winter."

"Naw, too much work. We're civilized men. We know enough about building to make us a decent cabin."

"My grandpa, when he came to Indiana, spent the first winter in a shelter that was half a cave cut into a hillside."

"Not opposed to the idea, Johnny. First we'll need to find a good spot though."

They let their eyes drift up and down stream, on both sides of the quiet river. The hot breeze dried the sweat from their thin shirts. John realized that conceptualizing The Plan had stirred and empowered Peter for the past year. It had impelled both of them this far into the heart of the continent.

Now would come the arduous task of realizing The Plan. John recognized how difficult it could be for two people to work in harmony on one plan, how easily it could lead to conflict. He doubted that Peter had even considered such a possibility.

The men spent the next few days paddling up the Heart, trying to get a sense of the river and the surrounding country. In the coulees they saw mule deer and, on the plains, herds of bison. They saw plentiful signs of the smaller animals they would be trapping in the winter. They still had not settled the issue of where to build their winter home. Peter grew snappier each day.

That evening, as the jackrabbits they'd shot earlier roasted on spits over the fire, John tried to lighten the mood. "It sure looks like we won't have to worry about going hungry this winter. Deer, buffalo, rabbits—we'll be eating like kings."

Peter grunted, "Yeah, I guess so. Haven't found a decent place for our shelter, though."

For days, John had been mulling a suggestion. He'd hesitated sharing it, fearing Peter's reaction. But, since The Plan seemed to have hit a snag, he decided to offer up his idea.

He spoke softly, "If we're going to be selling our furs to the French trappers up by the Mandan village, might it not make sense to settle our shelter up in that direction? Instead of out here alone on the Heart, we'd be just a few miles up the Missouri near other people." John looked up and saw Peter scowling.

"Other people…drunken Frenchies, lazy Indians and their squaws… I don't need to be close to those other people. Maybe you do, but…." He growled, and spat into the fire. "That ain't part of My Plan. Are we gonna get up every morning and cross miles of country to check our traps just cuz you need to be close to them savages?"

John waved his hand, "Whoa Peter, I was just sharing an idea. We seemed to be stuck on where to build our shelter. Thought I'd toss out my two bits."

Peter pulled one of the spits off the fire and began tearing off chunks of blackened meat. Between bites he muttered, "We'll build against that hillside across the river fifty yards upstream. We can dig into the hill, just like your grandpa did. We'll start tomorrow."

As John chewed on the stringy rabbit meat, he silently nodded. At least he'd managed to move the Plan forward.

*　　　　*　　　　*

The first yellow leaves of autumn were cartwheeling into the river in the September breeze as the two men paddled downstream toward the Missouri. They reached the mouth of the Heart and headed upstream toward the Mandan village. John's spirits were as high as the puffy clouds sailing in the azure sky.

After weeks of labor, he and Peter had finally finished building their cabin. The back end was buried six feet into the hillside and another six feet of rough log walls extended out facing the river bank fifty feet away. The shelter was topped by a roof of cottonwood saplings covered with squares of sod.

As they dug into the hillside, downed trees, and trimmed branches, John learned that Peter might adopt any of his suggestions but only if they were presented as options to be considered. Peter needed to feel that all decisions were part of His Plan. John had learned when to speak and when to shut up. This morning, he grinned as he dug his paddle into the muddy water. He was looking forward to seeing other faces and hearing other voices.

They'd been paddling northeastward for less than an hour, when they saw women harvesting corn in fields on the flatlands. A few minutes later, the village came into view. John remembered hearing the people call their home "Mintutanka" but Clark's expedition maps read "Matootohna." Whatever its name it, its forty round earthen lodges stood proudly on a plain fifty feet above the water.

A cluster of children stood on the shore as the men paddled up. Peter muttered as they pulled the canoe onto the bank, "Well, looks like the tribe's still alive. I'm hopin' they've got a horse to trade. If Big White is still chief here, maybe he'll remember us and not try to cheat us too bad."

John barely registered his partner's grousing. He was remembering the long winter months they'd spent near this village, and the occasional visits they'd all made to the lodges. Now he was scanning the crowd of chattering young boys and girls. He looked for those who might be six years old, those whose skin and hair might be lighter than their peers. He thought he saw one or two that fit that description but couldn't be sure. He grinned ruefully. *Maybe I'm just imagining…a wisp of wishful thinking.*

They climbed the path to the village, accompanied by the children running barefoot and giggling with excitement. Peter marched directly toward the central lodge while John lingered with the children trying to remember the few words of Mandan he'd learned seven winters ago.

A white-bearded old man, dressed in a striped shirt and wearing a red wool cap sat cross-legged in front of the lodge. He spoke in broken English with a French accent.

"Ah, the Americans from the east come again."

Peter stopped, took off his hat, and bowed, "Only two of us this time, Mr. René."

Though Peter and John had never been part of the Expedition's important meetings during their long winter with the Mandans, they and all the other men knew of the French trapper Rene Jusseaume, who'd lived for nearly two decades with the Mandans, spoke their language and had done interpreting for Lewis and Clark.

The elderly man slowly got to his feet. "Hope you bring no sickness with you. Last year hunters, they come upriver. One month later, forty peoples dead of the grippe."

Peter shook his head, "We're not sick and we aren't staying here. My name is Peter Weiser and this is my partner, John Thompson. We've built a cabin on the Heart and plan to trap on that river this winter. We came to speak with Chief Big White and barter for a horse."

René combed gnarled fingers through his scraggly beard, "This be difficult challenge. Big White he die from the grippe in past winter."

As he spoke a short, stocky man stepped out of the lodge and crossed his arms across his chest and glared at the two men.

René turned to the man and spoke for a few minutes in Mandan. The man responded but kept his eyes fixed on Peter and John.

René said to the two, "This man, he is Little Raven. Now is the chief. I tell him about your plans. He say you are free to trap furs on the Heart, but he has no horses for trading."

"But we've not even said what we could offer," Peter sputtered. Little Raven spun around and reentered the lodge. René shrugged, blinked slowly, and gave the men a wry grin.

Peter turned and with his back to the Frenchman, growled so only John could hear, "This insolent French bastard. We don't know what he told that Indian and we don't know what the Indian said. Shit."

Without a backward glance Peter began marching back across the open square toward the trail down the side of the mesa toward the river. John hurried to catch up with him, "Maybe we could head upriver, cross over to east bank, to that other village…"

Peter was fuming, "Screw it. Screw 'em all. We don't need a horse and we don't need the damn Indians. And next spring when we pack up our bundles of furs, I sure as hell ain't going to let that Frenchman make me an offer. Before I do that, I'll take 'em myself down to St. Louis."

Wait..How does that square with The Plan? Where do I fit in? How will I… John's questions went unasked. Peter was already clambering to the stern of their canoe and ferociously gripping his paddle with white-knuckled hands. He was clearly in no mood for conversation.

*   *   *

"Honk, honk, honk." The nasal, one syllable tone filled the late October sky.

Peter and John pulled their paddles from the water and watched the ragged vee of geese heading south. They'd been seeing and hearing these Canada geese by the tens of thousands for at least eight weeks. But since the first dusting of snow a week ago, they hadn't seen any of them.

"Those must be the lazy ones," Peter chuckled and resumed paddling upstream. "They better get their feathered asses outta here before the blizzards come."

The two men had spent the past month preparing food for the long winter ahead. They'd shot a buffalo and dried some of it into jerky. They were lucky to find some late chokecherries and had combined those with pulverized jerky and buffalo fat into balls of pemmican. And, despite Peter's fiery words in September, they'd returned to the Mandan village and traded some knives for a dozen bushels of corn. They planned on hunting throughout winter for fresh game as needed.

For the past few days they'd been preparing the metal traps they'd brought with them upriver. Their future fortune depended on these twelve spring traps. Back in St. Louis, early in the year, as they were discussing The Plan, Peter had questioned John.

"Do you know anything about trapping?"

John shrugged, "Well, I saw some men going out to trap that winter on the Expedition. But me personally? Only a little. My uncle did some trapping of rabbits and I'd go with him sometimes to check his snares."

Peter waved his hand dismissively, "Naw, snaring rabbits ain't trapping. We'll be using metal foothold traps, the kind with a flat pan that holds open the jaws until the critter steps in, then 'whap'." He slammed his meaty hands together. "The jaws clamp on its leg and hold on until we show up. You know what I'm talking about?"

John had seen the traps and generally understood how they worked. He knew he was not a trapper but was sure he could learn.

Peter pressed his would-be companion, "If we're going to be partners, and share in the riches, we gotta share in the investment. I've got me eight traps and a canoe. What can you come up with?"

John had saved some money from his shipping job and had a horse back on his father's farm. By the time they'd embarked on their voyage in April he'd gathered enough cash to purchase four traps, cooking equipment and knives for trading. Peter had accepted John's investment, though both men knew from the beginning who was junior and who was senior in their partnership.

Now, six months later and a thousand miles north of their starting point, they were only beginning the labor they hoped would make them rich. On this October day they were setting out their trapline.

Earlier in the fall, they'd carefully searched for game trails and burrows in the river and creek banks. John had made a rough map of the sites that seemed most promising. Now as they paddled up river, he consulted his drawing. "There, where the willows hang over the bank, there's a spot you thought looked good." They paddled to a sandy beach, pulled up the canoe and walked carefully, trying not to disturb the trail of pressed down grass running along the water's edge.

John carried a trap wrapped in a piece of buffalo hide, following Peter who was examining the trail.

Peter stopped, "Here, where there's a dip, we'll set the first one. Unwrap it, but don't touch it."

When they'd disembarked from the canoe, Peter had grabbed a handful of mud and sand and scoured his hands. Now he opened up a pouch on his belt and pulled out ashes from last night's campfire. As he rubbed the ashes on the jaws of the trap he said, "We'll have no furs or fortune unless we trick these critters' noses."

John watched intently as Peter drove a stake into deep into the earth and attached it to the trap's chain. Then he carefully opened the jaws of the trap and set the pan in place. Finally, he sprinkled grass lightly over the trap. They stood for a moment examining their work.

Peter murmured, "Tonight, when Mrs. Mink comes trotting down this trail, if we're lucky, she'll be in a hurry and not notice the tiny change in her usual pathway and then, if we're lucky, she'll put her foot in the right place, and if we're lucky, the jaws will snap in the right spot, and if we're lucky, she'll be caught, and if we're lucky, a coyote won't find her before we do….Ah Johnny boy… We'll need all that luck and then some…"

The men picked their way cautiously back to the canoe and spent the rest of the day setting their trapline and imagining the fortune they would harvest in the months ahead.

*   *   *

In mid-December the temperature plummeted far below zero and, in the eight weeks since then, it barely climbed into the single digits, even on the days when the sun managed to shine. Tonight, the wind was howling like a thousand demons. The biting Arctic air penetrated every chink in their little cabin but Peter and John were surprisingly warm. Not only were they both fully dressed and each rolled up in a buffalo robe, they'd also indulged in Peter Weiser's whiskey. At least Peter had indulged. He'd shared only a shot glass full with John while he had enjoyed a half dozen deep gulps.

Peter laughed into the darkness, "Johnny boy, that stack of furs outside, she's piling up damn fine. By spring, when we sell 'em, we'll be flush."

John too was pleased by the sleek, beautiful pelts they'd accumulated. But the matter of where and how the selling of them would happen hadn't been settled. That question was like a nettle stuck in his sock. It didn't always bother him, it never overpowered him, but neither did it disappear. More than once he'd try to broach the matter, but Peter would brusquely change the subject. And John knew that tonight, huddled against the howling blizzard, with a half-drunk partner, was no time to bring up the matter. Instead he spoke of their latest catch.

"Wasn't that mink I brought in this afternoon a beauty?" John had marveled at the fur, so thick and lustrous it seemed to radiate warmth.

Peter chuckled, "She must have been a hot little bitch. Reminds me of those squaws that winter in the Mandan village. If you got them in the dark, they went at it like minks in heat."

John lay silently, peering into the black night. Then he quietly asked, "Did you ever go to their buffalo calling ceremony?"

"Their what?"

"The ceremony when they danced and called out for spirit power so the buffalo hunt would be successful."

Peter belched, "Who the hell could figure out what those dumb savages were up to. My head was usually spinnin' from the whiskey and all their whirlin' didn't help none. When some squaw in heat opened up her door, and her legs, I didn't ask why."

A memory was etched in John's mind, a memory he would not, could not share with Peter. Six years ago, late in March, only a few weeks before the Expedition left its winter encampment, a feverish spirit hummed throughout the Mandan village. One of the French traders explained to some of the men what was setting the tribe abuzz.

"Tonight, you will see the buffalo calling ceremony. Drums, dancing…The tribe calls on spirit power, help to kill many buffalo." And then with a salacious wink he added a comment that John understood only later.

"The braves, the hunters, they see you boys as strong medicine. They think, maybe you bring strong spirit power to their lodge. You boys, better you be ready for a warm night."

When evening came, the air cooled but retained a hint of the balmy springtime soon to come. John and several dozen other men from the Expedition sat with their backs against the lodges as the tribe gathered in the central plaza. Some of the Mandan men and women had dressed in decorated deerskin and were slowly circling to the sound of rattles and drums. They began dancing and spinning as the beat grew louder.

One of the men stepped out of the circle and came toward John and his friends. He was tall, regal and solemn. He stopped directly in front of John and gestured for him to stand. When John stood, the man bowed deeply and then waved for John to follow. Never during their long months with the Mandan had there been any sense of danger, so John was not afraid. But his pulse raced as he followed this serious man striding across the plaza.

They came to the entrance of one of the lodges. Standing in the doorway was a woman. John presumed she was the man's wife. She was nearly as tall as John with lustrous long hair parted in the middle and lying upon her shoulders. She wore a deerskin robe fringed with feathers. Her eyes were luminous and dark. The man looked into her face, she nodded and held out her hand. Then, the man took John's hand and placed it in hers. John questioningly looked at the man who simply nodded and pointed to the doorway. John felt a tug. The woman, with bright eyes and a small smile was pulling him into the lodge. John shot a glance back and saw the man face toward the plaza, cross his arms and stand guard in front of the entrance.

By the flickering embers of a fire in the center of the lodge, John could see the woman was leading him to a pile of robes in the dark corner. When they reached it, she began lifting her robe over her head. He was a healthy young man, and no virgin, but knowing that the head of the clan, the husband of this woman was standing outside the door…a fearful wave of anxiety swept over him.

*   *   *

Six years after that night, John lay in the tiny cabin. Outside was the roar of the howling blizzard. Inside were the snores of his trapping partner. But despite all the noise, he could hear again her soft murmurs, feel once more her calm, gentle caresses, the smoothness of her neck beneath his kisses, the sweet hardness of her nipples against his chest and the fierce strength of her arms as she pulled him into herself.

Peter's words about the Mandan women had not only angered John. They'd offended him. In his memory, the hours in that lodge had been a sacred experience. He would never know if his presence that night gave this couple any spirit power, strong medicine, or success in the hunt. He did know that those hours would flavor his dreams for as long as he lived.

*   *   *

John slogged up to the entrance of their cabin. Early in the day he'd gone north to check their traps. Then, after dropping off the catch at their cabin, had gone south to check the rest of their sets. Now as the feeble, late February sun was sliding toward the horizon, he heaved a grateful sigh. He dropped his bag on the packed snow in front of the door and entered the dim room.

"Only one lousy muskrat from the south line. Damn my toes are cold."

Peter, huddled in a buffalo robe, was chewing jerky and sitting on one of their makeshift stools. Between chews he grunted, "The season's headin' toward the end. Maybe three, four more weeks. Still, it was a good day. That beaver you brought in this morning was a beauty. Fine pelt, prime one, I'd say. Prob'ly worth $6 or more."

"You mean you've already skinned it?" John asked.

"Course I did. Skinned it, fleshed it and already stretched it. I ain't just sittin' here while you're out."

John wearily lowered himself onto the other stool. "I was hoping I could watch you."

Peter shrugged, "No need for that. You do the fetchin', I do the rest."

"But I'd like to learn how you do it. I think I should know."

Peter scowled, "And why do you think you should know?"

John leaned forward, "If we're trapping partners, we should both know the business. That way we can share the work."

Peter waved dismissively, "You don't need to know to prepare the skins. That's my job. Your job is to check the trap line and bring in the pelts. That's what we decided."

The long, bleak winter and the day's weariness had shrunk John's inherent patience. He clenched his jaw. "That's what you decided. I didn't know how to prepare the skins so I had no choice. I'm saying you could teach me how to do it, so we could divide up the work evenly."

Peter's eyes grew dark, he pulled at his scraggly black beard and gruffly responded, "You came in with a few traps, and no experience but I took you on. And by God, you signed on to The Plan. I'm a trapper, not your damn teacher. We're a trapping partnership. That's The Plan."

John sprang up from his seat, "The Plan, The Plan. You keep flinging out 'The Plan' as if it was carved in stone like the Ten Commandments. Sure, I agreed to your ideas when we started out. But along the way, you always decide what works best for you, and then announce that it's The Plan."

Peter glowered and growled, "Are you callin' me a cheater?"

Exasperated, John threw his hands into the air. "No, I didn't say you were a cheater. I'm saying that The Plan always ends up being what works best for you. I never get a vote."

Peter began to speak but John cut him off with a torrent of words that had been festering for months. "What happens come spring? What're we gonna do with the pelts. Last year, when we left St. Louis, you told me we were going to sell 'em to the Frenchies at the Mandan village. That was The Plan. Then in the fall, you got pissed off and swore you'd never let that French trader even see your pelts. So now what? We got a stack of furs, but they aren't worth shit without a buyer."

Peter stood and the buffalo robe fell to the dirt floor. His voice was icy steel. He thumped his chest, "I'm the trapper. I've got the experience. I've got the connections." He crossed his arms across his chest, "Some traders are bound to be comin' upriver this spring. I heard 'em talking in St. Louis last year. When the ice goes out, we can decide if we'll go meet 'em, or wait for 'em to get here."

"We can decide? Or you can decide?" John shook his head at the futility of the argument. He turned and stepped outside. The pale sun was surrendering to the Arctic night and bathing the landscape in an icy blue. High in the hills, across the river a coyote howled plaintively. In the brittle evening air, John's anger slowly chilled, leaving behind only a residue of resignation.

*   *   *

John's deerskin shirt was sweat-soaked as he trudged along the banks of the river. The last days of March had seen a rapid shift in weather. Last night it had rained and now puddles dappled the cracked ice on the Heart. Mare's tail clouds high in the sky hinted that more moisture was on the way.

At dawn, Peter had stood in the doorway of the cabin and declared, "Trappin' season is over. We better pull in our traps before the ice goes out. Wouldn't surprise me if upriver there ain't already ice jams threatenin' to bust open. You fetch the north ones, I'll go south."

John was carrying the sack full of traps over his shoulder. Besides their weight, he was bearing another more onerous burden. Since expressing his frustration a month ago, he and Peter had spoken only when necessary. John feared his remarks had only served to harden Peter's single-mindedness. As he puffed along the river bank he mulled over his limited options for the months ahead.

Suddenly he jerked to a halt, let the sack clank to the ground, and slapped his forehead. *Damn it, I forgot to pull trap #3. I can just imagine Peter's sneer if I come back one trap short...*

John left the bag where he'd dropped it and began a slow jog through the slushy snow. Ten minutes later he arrived at the bank overlooking the site. The river ice was laced with cracks and on the far side, John could see a silvery band of running water. He slid down the muddy slope to the narrow game trail that ran next to the ice. Because the winter's frost was leaving the ground, he had no trouble pulling out the stake. He held onto the chain and began scrambling up the incline. His foot slipped in the mud and as he tried to catch his balance lost his grip on the trap. It tumbled down the slope and skittered ten feet out onto the ice.

With a weary sigh and a muttered curse, he slid back down and stepped cautiously onto the ice. As he planted his full weight on the pitted surface, without so much as a warning crack, his feet plunged down into the water. He managed to throw his hands out and keep his waist on the ice. He lay stretched out, gasping at the stabbing chill. He was stunned by the current that was tugging at his legs with icy tenacity.

He tried to wriggle forward, and had managed to pull himself out almost to his knees, when a crack appeared in front of him and the entire ice chunk began to lift. His frozen fingers found a tiny crevice and he was able to keep from slipping completely into the frigid dark waters.

Then, above his own frantic panting he heard a sound: A dull grinding, grumbling noise, as if logs were rolling over stones. He looked over his shoulder and his heart froze.

Somewhere upstream, the Heart River ice had cracked and begun moving. Ice floes, bigger than their cabin had spun and tumbled in the Arctic water.

Then, at a narrow bend in the river, those floes had been jammed together and formed a ragged dam. The icy waters in upstream creeks and springs, set free by last night's rain, continued to race gleefully into the river and press relentlessly against the frigid dam. Finally, with a creaking groan the dam had given way, and now a maelstrom of ice chunks, and foaming water a yard high was roaring downstream toward John.

He made a frenzied scramble to the front edge of the ice chunk, just as the wall of water hit him. He felt a sharp lift and for a moment thought he would ride above the wave. But the churning water bucked and then tumbled him into the frozen slurry. He leaned back and tried to keep his face above water. He could no longer feel his body. He stared up into the wispy veiled blue Dakota sky and surrendered.

His thoughts flickered. *Lost one trap, Peter will be pissed. He won't miss me…All the furs are his now. This river is as cold and relentless as him and his damn plan…Don't suppose I'll float down to St. Louis…Probably sink and get pushed into the mud somewhere downstream.*

Icy tendrils began to wrap around his brain and his last thoughts were warm: the embrace of a Mandan maid, and the sunshine on his chubby cheeks as he sat on his mother's lap. He gasped once, then quietly slipped beneath the frothing water and was gone.

*   *   *

Samson gasped, jerked in his lawn chair, and the skull rolled onto the grass. Its dark empty eyes stared up into the sunlight filtering through the leaves. Samson felt the blood throbbing in his throat, his heart thundering in his chest. A sound filled his ears, the sound of raging waters. With a trembling hand he reached for the beer bottle. The glass was still cool. His mind was addled.

How?… Mere minutes have passed…but I saw, I lived…a year…not possible…yet…it all was so real…so vivid..so…

When the roaring sound left his ears and his heart slowed, Samson eased himself out of the chair. He cautiously picked up the skull, careful to not look into its dark eye sockets. He gently placed it into the battered box. On shaky legs he walked back to the garage and returned the box to its niche below the workbench.

He stepped back out into the sunlight. He was befuddled but beneath his perplexity another current surged, something he could not yet name: Apprehension? Disquiet? Fear?

Samson's mind was overtaken by roiling thoughts. But, as they'd done so often when he was overwhelmed with growing up, his feet carried him toward the banks of the Heart River. He numbly walked until, with a start, his eyes cleared and he stared down into the summer-slow current of the river. He was a nearly a mile away from the farmstead and a hundred and fifty years away from the present in his mind.

He labored to comprehend what he had just experienced. *How did this vision come to me? How was I carried to that space and time? How was time compressed? Mystifying, Unexplainable.*

He threw sticks into the water and watched them drift lazily downstream. He wandered in the short, dry grass along the banks and inevitably resorted to the categories and disciplines he'd been studying and teaching for nearly two decades.

What a story—interesting plot, setting, and characters. Were I to assign it to my students, what questions would I ask them? Maybe: are the characters believable? Is its genre historical fiction? This is the story of two men. Who tells the story? What is the point of view?

As he mulled over that last question, the submerged anxiety he'd felt earlier bobbed to the surface of his consciousness.

POV, point of view. How often I've lectured on its importance, tried to impress upon my students how POV gives shapes and flavor to the narrative. Haven't I told them that if you change the point of view you alter the story in dramatic ways?

A hot breeze sprang up and sent ripples against the current. Samson stared at the glinting water and gulped as the question forced itself upon his mind: *Samson Bartz, from whose point of view has the story of your marriage been written?*

*   *   *

That evening, Samson sat on the back-porch steps, welcoming the westerly breeze that kept the mosquitoes from attacking. From the living room inside the house, he could hear the muted tones of Johnny Carson on the Tonight Show, part of his parents' nightly ritual. From downstairs, thankfully, he heard nothing.

His children had returned from their fishing trip exuberant and sun-burned. They'd helped Uncle John clean their catch of fish and watched their grandpa grill them. After supper, Samson had gone downstairs, rubbed their necks and arms with cooling lotion and tucked them into bed. Lillian had smiled sleepily up at him and sunk like a stone into slumber. But Jeff and Sammy squirmed and giggled, still electrified by the day's adventures. Samson had made three trips downstairs and issued ever sterner warnings. Now all was quiet and he assumed they were asleep.

He stared into the velvet darkness. The steady chirping of crickets filled the night, the mating call of lonely males. He was as restless and as charged as his two boys had been. The events of his day continued to churn and tumble in his mind. He felt confused and on edge.

"Enjoying the breeze?" Helen softly asked, speaking through the screen door.

"Yeah...I guess."

"You seemed awfully quiet tonight. Feeling OK?"

Samson sighed, "Ahh Mom, you know me. I'm always mulling over something."

Only cricket chirping filled the next few moments. Then Helen quietly spoke, "Anything I can help with?"

Samson grabbed his knees and abruptly embraced what he'd been trying to avoid. "Mom, I'd like you and Dad to take care of the kids for a few days. Could you do that?"

Helen stepped out of house and sat down on the cooling concrete steps beside her son. "Well, sure, I guess so...what's up?"

He looked up into the inky sky before speaking. "Mom, I think I need to work on some things with Diane and...and, well, I...we can't do that with the kids around..." He silently prayed his mother would not ask any questions.

She simply laid her hand on his knee. "Of course, when will you go?"

Relieved by her response, and by having finally reached his own decision, he quickly replied, "Tomorrow, early. I'll drive straight through. In a few days, hopefully, the two of us will come back and fetch our brood."

Helen rubbed his knee then slowly stood, "Then you better get some sleep, Son. Don't worry about the kids. I'll tell them you have some work to do, which is true, I suppose. We'll keep them occupied until you and Diane pick them up."

She quietly went inside. Samson stood, took a deep breath, and hoped he'd be able to unwind enough to settle down.

*   *   *

The tinny rattle of his travel alarm snapped him awake. He quickly turned it off and sat up. 5AM. The decision he'd reached last night had alleviated enough of his anxiety to allow him to sleep. But now adrenaline raced through his system. He grabbed the suitcase he'd packed last night and hurried out to the kitchen. His parents were sitting at the table sipping coffee. He was not surprised.

Roland asked, "Got enough gas? You could take some from the bulk fuel tank before you go."

"Thanks Dad, but I'm good. I'll stop in Bismarck, fill the tank and grab a donut." Samson took the coffee cup his mother held out to him, and gave her a hug. He felt his throat swell with tears, "You guys...thank you so much...I'll, I'll see you in a few days. I'll let you know."

He stepped out into the chill air of early morning. Sunrise was still a half hour away but the eastern horizon already bore the pale tints of dawn when he pulled out of his parent's farmyard. Gravel rattled against the bottom of the car for the first ten miles. The abrupt silence when he reached the blacktop state highway only served to accentuate the thoughts clattering in Samson's mind.

Samson recognized that the vividness of yesterday's vision was beginning to fade. Much like in a dream--the colors, sounds, words—the entire experience, was becoming less substantial, more translucent. But what persisted, what grew more solid and real in Samson's mind, was the awareness that in his mystical episode he'd been looking at the world through the eyes of another person. And, he was painfully and acutely conscious of one factor: that person's destiny was to a great extent determined by someone else.

Point of view, point of view…the story depends on whose eyes we are invited to employ. What would our life story look like if I saw it through Diane's eyes?

The first rays of the morning sun greeted him as the Volvo crested a hill. He snapped down the sun visor but then the road swooped down into the unlit valley. For the next few minutes, as he traveled over the rolling landscape, he witnessed the sunrise over and over again. By the time he reached the four-lane interstate highway, the sun had conquered all of the hills and he drove straight into relentless illumination. He gripped the wheel with both hands, squinted ahead, and asked himself, *Do I have the courage, the right, to even try to see what she might have seen in our history? How might our first year have looked through **her** eyes?*

*　　　　*　　　　*

Diane, still warm from her shower, emerged from the bathroom, wrapped in her robe. Today was the day of the big interview. She smiled to herself. *I know it's not 'big,big', but it's my first real shot at a job as a new graduate. And the food bank is such a wholesome, grounded place.*

She pulled a couple of blouses out of their tiny bedroom closet and laid them out on the bed. *What to wear for a job interview as a community outreach leader at a food bank?*

She held one of the blouses in front of her and posed in front of the mirror.

She heard the phone ring out in the living room, then a few minutes later Samson called her.

"Hey Di, come out here please."

Still holding the blouse, she stepped out of the bedroom and saw her husband, arms stretched out across the top of their battered couch, grinning with delight.

"Guess who just called?"

She grinned back at him and simply shrugged.

He leapt to his feet and wrapped his arms around her. "It was the Grad School Director of the U of M English Department. I'm in, I'm in. I was accepted into their grad program, starting in September. Minneapolis, here we come!" He picked her up and they swung in a circle.

"Oh Samson, that's awesome. I'm so glad for you. All your hard work, I knew you'd make it." She kissed him, released herself from his grip and let her practical mind begin to ask questions.

"Is there student housing or will we need to find an apartment? Will you get a stipend? What will I do? Should I start applying for jobs? Wow. So many details. Guess we better start packing."

"Yeah, right. Geez. I'm going to run over to Charlie's apartment real quick and tell him the good news." He flew out the door and thundered down the stairs.

Diane stood for a moment in the empty living room, still holding the blouse in her hand. *Minneapolis, grad school. Of course. We agreed. That's been the plan all along.*

She moved slowly into the bedroom. *Guess I better call the food bank and cancel. Common courtesy.* She sighed, *I'm sure they'll find someone else.*

She didn't bother hanging up the blouse. She laid it down beside the other one, pulled the suitcase out from under the bed and started packing.

*   *   *

Samson pulled into the Chevron station on the outskirts of Bismarck. He'd just passed Mandan, where the Heart River entered the Missouri and then crossed over the Memorial Bridge that spanned the Big Muddy. After filling his gas tank, he stepped inside the convenience store. He bought a donut, a cup of coffee and picked up a pair of cheap sunglasses. His head already hurt from squinting into the glaring sun. He ruefully grinned to himself, *Or, maybe the ache comes from looking at life through another set of eyes.*

He merged onto the freeway then looked at his watch. It was 7:30AM and he had almost an eight-hour drive ahead. The freeway shot like an arrow across the state. When he reached the Minnesota border, he would begin to see trees and lakes. Until then, it was mile after mile of potholes and prairie, a long slog. Slog... an apt description of his five years of graduate work. *What words would Diane use to tell the story of those five years?*

*   *   *

Samson finished a round of thank you's and then said, "I'd like my dear wife Diane to come up here and join me."

They had reserved the activity room in their apartment complex for Samson's graduation party. As she looked out over the room, she saw the many people who'd filled her life during these past five years. Diane smiled through a film of tears and only barely heard her husband's words.

"Diane has been my steady rock in the midst of the grad school flood. She doesn't get flustered and more than once pulled me up when I was sinking."

Samson went on, stacking metaphor upon metaphor, but Diane was focusing on the faces. She was secretly proud, not of the support she'd given her husband. That was part of her calling as a wife. Society expected that of her and she expected it of herself. What filled her with hidden joy was that when they'd sent out invitations to this party, it was her colleagues, her friends who'd responded. Two of Samson's fellow students were here, and one of his professors. And of course, Helen and Roland had made the trip for the graduation and the party. But the rest…with gleaming eyes Diane silently thanked them one by one.

Samantha, my co-manager at the bakery, you convinced me I could do it. Eunice, Karla and Joe, you kept me sane dealing with those crazy junior highers. And Bill and Doris, Warren and Allie, choir buddies, your laughter and embraces helped fill so many lonely evenings.

After the speeches, the room buzzed with conversations as people chatted and nibbled on the sandwiches Diane and Helen had prepared. The two women stood behind the serving table making sure the trays were full.

"Sorry your parents couldn't make it," Helen said.

Diane shrugged, "Dairy farmers are slaves to those cows. Morning and evening, every day. I grew up with it. Learned to live with it."

Helen put her arm around her daughter-in-law's waist and gave her a gentle hug. "Dear, I know you did much more than just support my son during these five years."

Diane, caught off guard by Helen's insight, swallowed the sudden lump in her throat and returned Helen's hug.

"Oh, yeah. The first year was tough though. Clearing tables, taking orders, putting up with all sorts of rude customers… I wondered what I'd gotten into. I more or less escaped to the bakery job, thought of it as just another time-filler. But Helen, you know I learned something about myself. When Samantha asked me to be day manager, I was scared. But I found out that I can handle pressure and manage people. I ended up having fun. When I finally was offered a job in my profession at the Junior High, I regretted saying goodbye to the bakery.

Helen nodded, "And now you have to say goodbye to everyone. That must be hard."

Diane sighed, blinked away tears, and gave Helen a smile. "For sure. All of these people who were part of my life for these five years…guess I'll be grieving for a while. Samson won't. He's relieved. He and I… we both knew this was a temporary stop, a part of the plan. And now we'll move to Wisconsin. He'll start teaching and I'll…." Her voice trailed off and she shrugged.

"You'll do just fine. I'm sure of it. And who knows," Helen dared give Diane a tiny tickle in her ribs, "maybe you could start a family." She grabbed an empty tray and headed toward the kitchen. She looked over her shoulder and winked, "I'm not opposed to being called a grandma."

*   *   *

Samson exited the freeway and pulled into the Fargo Country Kitchen parking lot. He slid into a booth and thanked the hostess as she handed him a menu. He scanned the daily specials then leaned back and watched the waitresses scurrying throughout the room.

Do any of them think of this job as their future? Doubt it…I wonder what dream they're chasing? A college degree? Tech school diploma? Whose plan are they supporting? Their own? A boyfriend's? A husband's?

"Ready to order?" the blond, pony-tailed waitress interrupted his ruminations. He was tempted to ask her the questions he'd been pondering but instead grinned and teased, "So, why no buffalo burger on your menu? Ever since I passed that giant bison statue along the freeway by Jamestown, I've been hankering buffalo meat."

She smiled and shot back, "You want buffalo, gotta go downtown to a fancy restaurant and pay an arm and a leg. Here, all we got is good old Dakota beef." She giggled, "Guess I shouldn't say the beef is old…Ready to order?"

"Sure, give me the Country Boy burger and ice tea." He handed her the menu and she hurried off to the kitchen.

Wisps from yesterday's vision floated in his mind. *No buffalo roaming and ice domesticated in plastic glasses, trappers mostly gone…but people still dream dreams, make plans. And we all take others with us on that journey. Dreams collide, plans overlap or diverge. How can I talk about this with Diane? Will she listen? Bigger question, will she talk?*

After lunch, back on the freeway, with his stomach full and the hum of the tires in his ears, Samson fought drowsiness. He opened his window, ratcheted the radio's volume to full blast and bit the inside of his cheek---anything to fight off sleep. As he struggled, he remembered the weariest years of their life together. He imagined how Diane might have seen those years...

*   *   *

She heard the back-door slam and rose from the rocker. When he walked into the living room, she was ready. Before he could even take off his jacket, she handed him the baby.

"Here. I'm going out for a walk. Jeffy is on the potty trying to poop. I just nursed Sammy and changed his diaper. I'll be back in a while."

Samson looked taken aback but she didn't wait for a response. She grabbed her coat, sped down the steps and began striding down the sidewalk.

Oh dear God, it's good to breathe. I love my boys, my precious boys. Don't even want to imagine life without them. But...

She reached the corner and turned westward. The brisk early March breeze struck her face and brought tears to her eyes.

But somedays I feel like I'm drowning, losing myself. I wanted to be a mother, wanted a family. We decided together. That was always the plan. And I love being a mother. I just never knew being a mother would swallow so much of me.

The beep of a car horn startled her. Jessica, one of the mom's in her babysitting co-op had just parked her car across the street. She emerged and gave Diane a wave before opening the car's back door to unbuckle her two-year-old from his car seat. Diane returned the wave then strode forward.

Jessica and the other moms...they keep me from sinking completely. But though I stay afloat, here in Janesville, I really don't have much of a name...either I'm Jeffrey and Sammy's mommy. Or I'm Professor Bartz's wife...

She reached the little neighborhood park. The grass was still brown and bleak, muddy puddles filled the low spots beneath the swings.

I can hardly wait for spring. Get out of the house, take the boys out for walks. Maybe Samson could come home early and take them out...they need more daddy time. I hope Jeffy'll be toilet trained by then...

Diane continued her hike around the park and headed home. Her breath came easier and she felt lighter as she entered the house. Samson sat on the couch holding Sammy. Jeffrey snuggled beside him engrossed in late afternoon cartoons.

"Brrr. Its chilly outside. Here are my boys, all cozy and warm," she smiled as she hung up her coat. As she walked to the kitchen, she teased, "And I suppose dinner is ready to be served?"

Samson grinned weakly, "Me, in the kitchen? And with the boys.."

"I know, I know. I've got a hotdish in the fridge. I'll stick it in the oven."

She was setting the oven temperature when Samson called, "How long will it take to heat up?"

Diane slid the pan into the oven then reentered the living room. "About forty-five minutes. Why do you ask?"

He hesitated for a moment. "The curriculum committee is meeting at 7."

Diane exhaled, "Another meeting. I don't know why you have to be on every committee your department creates."

Samson tensed, and bounced the baby on his knee. "I'm doing what I can to be a team player. If anyone ever looks at my resumé, if we ever want to move up from Whitewater College…" His voice trailed off as Diane turned around and reentered the kitchen.

As she set the plates and silverware on the kitchen table, she murmured, "Moving up and moving on …I guess that's always part of the plan."

*   *   *

Samson pulled off the freeway into the rest area. He visited the restroom then walked down the sidewalk between the pines. He twisted and arched his back, trying to loosen cramped muscles.

Attempting to gaze at life through Diane's eyes is stressful business. And maybe I'm totally deluded, presumptuous. Maybe I'm treading on thin ice to even venture it. Can I submerge my story and let hers rise? Can two stories co-exist?

His legs felt wooden as he dragged himself back to the car. Home stretch…The traffic would be intense as he neared Minneapolis. He punched the buttons on the radio, searching for music that could pacify the maelstrom in his mind. But then, he turned off the radio and decided to mentally compose a story of how Diane might have experienced their last move.

*   *   *

Diane's thoughts tumbled and pitched recklessly. To calm herself she grabbed her trowel and bucket from the garage and hurried to her refuge, her garden. It had taken all of their seven years in Winona to bring the soil in this vegetable garden to this deep, rich loamy consistency. Shortly after their arrival, she'd had some dirt brought in. But mostly, she'd managed this herself. By composting leaves, clippings and kitchen waste she'd managed to create this black gold. Two months ago, she'd set out cabbage and tomato sets and planted beets and carrots. She knelt beside a row of carrots and began to loosen the soil and pull out the thin plants.

"What're you doing Mom?" Jeffrey asked. He'd left his brother and sister playing in the sandbox and now knelt beside her.

Diane responded with a sigh, "Digging out the carrots."

"But they're not very big. Aren't they still growing?"

"Oh, they'd grow some more. But in a week we're moving. The new owners won't be coming until August so no one will be watering them or picking them. Might as well use what we can before we go." She thumped a handful of carrots into her bucket.

Jeffrey wiggled and tugged at a carrot top. "Mom, I don't want to move. All my friends are here. And my school."

The tears in his voice triggered her own. She sat back on her heels and swiped at her cheeks with her sleeve. "I know Jeffie, I know. It won't be easy for any of us."

"But why do we have to go?"

"Honey, you know why. It's because of your dad's job."

"But he has a job here, doesn't he?" He was hiding his tears behind anger.

Diane tried to sound convincing, "Yes, but the job in Minneapolis is a better job, a more important job."

Her thoughtful and troubled ten-year-old was not satisfied. "He'll still be teaching English, won't he? Just like here?"

Diane sensed she was losing ground in this discussion. "Well, sure. But, the U of M is an important school and not everyone gets to teach there and Daddy will get paid a little more and…" She threw her arm around her son and squeezed, "Wait till you see the new house and the trees in the back yard. I'm sure we can make a tree house for you and Sammy."

He gave her a weak smile. "And what about a garden, Mom? Will you have another garden?"

She stood and pulled him up and grabbed the bucket full of half-grown carrots. As they walked back to the house, she said, "We'll see. There's a lot of shade and I think the soil is pretty poor. It would take a lot of work, don't know if I want to start over…"

Jeff slowly walked back to the sandbox and she stood in the doorway. She pulled her eyes away from her garden and lawn. She pushed away the images of the rooms behind her that she'd so enthusiastically decorated. She closed the door on thoughts of the job she was leaving. She focused her eyes and her heart on her three children. *They'll be all right. In the fall, once school starts, they'll be fine. New friends, new teams. They're all that matters. In the end, they're all that matters. They'll be fine.*

*   *   *

Samson waited at the stop light a few blocks from home. He tried to breathe deeply but his chest seemed to have shrunk. Last night's decision to travel all this way, a decision driven by an unexplainable vison, now seemed hare-brained, so out of character. The car behind him honked as the light changed. He crept forward.

Maybe that's what I need...to get out of character. Or find a new side to my character. I can't rewrite my story...but I could write a new chapter, maybe...a story about starting over....

He pulled into the driveway and stopped the car. Diane was at the door, came out on the step, panic painting her face. He hurried up the walk and stood looking up at her.

"Honey, the kids are fine. They're on the farm. I came because...because I love you and we need to...No, I need to....I need to listen."

He stepped up, embraced her and quietly they cried together.

VISIONS FROM THE HEART
PART THREE: "Visions"

John Bartz opened his front door and greeted his brother, "Happy birthday, old man."

Seventy-year-old Samson stepped slowly into his brother's embrace, "You're not too far behind. Better watch your tongue."

"Hey, 'old man' is a sign of respect. Aren't elders considered the wise ones?"

Samson entered the living room, appreciating his brother's banter but unable to join in. "Maybe amongst the Chinese, or once upon a time for the Sioux and the Mandan. But, nowadays... mostly I just feel out of it... and old." He lowered himself wearily onto the couch. "Where's Susan?"

"She's doing yoga. She claims it keeps her young. Imagine, even here in Bismarck we've now got a half dozen yoga studios. Just like in the Twin Cities."

"Ha. We've got them in every strip mall, almost as thick as the coffee shops."

John settled into what was clearly his personal easy chair and sighed, "So sorry to hear about Diane. How's she adapting?"

Samson dropped his head, then raised bloodshot eyes and said softly, "Adapting...don't know if I'd use that word...No one really adapts to the Alzheimer's unit...Is there a better term? Adjusting, coping, reconciling..." He swiped at his eyes. "Sorry. Old English teacher's nemesis, trying to solve things with words…She's settling in. Guess I'm the one that needs to adapt."

"Seems like it all went so fast. Three years ago, at Lillian's wedding, she seemed fine."

"Even then, I knew something wasn't right. She did too. She'd start making a dessert she'd made a hundred times before and then forget what do to. Or she'd ask me a question and then ten minutes later ask the same question again. We both tried to pretend it was just ordinary aging."

"So, you finally convinced her to see a doctor?"

"Oh, no. Diane decided." Samson's voice grew tremulous. "She was so brave. She insisted on knowing everything…what to expect, her timeline, her…" He stopped and shook his head.

"So, how…when did you decide to…?" John paused.

"Put her in the care unit? Well, we'd talked about it early on. I said I'd take care of her at home. But from the start she'd said that if she ever started wandering or if she became paranoid, I should take her to the Unit. She didn't want me to have to lock her up or fight with her.

"Yeah, I guess that sounds like Diane, always thinking of others."

"Johnny, that's always how she was. So full of caring…. Anyway, about month ago, I was in the living room, she was in the kitchen, still in her pajamas." Samson shook his head at the memory.

"She went out the back door, into the alley and just started walking. A few minutes later I noticed she was gone. I ran outside, panicked, calling for her. My cell phone rang. Three blocks away, a lady saw her and thank God managed to get her to stop. She saw the wrist band I'd put on Diane's arm with my phone number on it. By the time I got there, Diane was sitting on the lady's front steps. When she saw me, she started whimpering, "Sorry, sorry…"

"Gosh, Samson, that's tough," John's own eyes teared up.

"Yeah, but it got worse. That night, around two o'clock I woke up and Diane was on her knees, peeking out of the window. She kept mumbling, "the devils, the devils…they're coming to get me." It took me an hour to calm her down."

John shook his head. "Sounds like the time had come."

Samson swallowed the lump in his throat. "Hardest thing I ever did, Johnny. Walked into that place holding her hand... The head nurse smiled and took her other hand... I had to let go. They walked away and Diane looked over her shoulder at me. The look in her eyes... Lost, like a lost little girlt. Fifty years last summer, we had fifty years...Now, I'm supposed to stay away for at least three weeks, while she settles in. That's why I decided to make this trip now." He rubbed his eyes with his palms.

A mournful silence pervaded the room. John tried to lighten the mood. "I hear your going to be a grandpa again."

Samson gave a weak smile. "Yeah, Lillian and Charles are expecting their first in November. That'll make six. Don't know if it's a boy or a girl. If they know, they haven't told us."

"What a blessing...having grandkids to spoil."

Samson knew that his brother and wife had long since come to terms with their own childlessness. He knew John's words were heartfelt and meant to be kind. But the leaden blanket of gloom pressed upon his spirit. "I guess. But they're all so far away, and so busy with their own lives. They don't have much use for an old, grumpy grandpa."

John, recognized the futility of the efforts to cheer up his brother. He resolved to answer the question Samson had posed on the phone yesterday, before he flew out from Minneapolis. "Susan and I talked last night. I don't think we'll go with you out to the farm. We said our good-byes to that place a decade ago, when we retired. All of the outbuildings are already gone, dismantled or moved away. Just the old house is left...guess it's falling apart. Bulldozer is coming next week. We want to remember it the way it was...Sorry."

Samson nodded. "It's OK. I understand. You guys spent your lives out there. I just feel like...like I need to say farewell, close the book." A wistful look crept across his features, "I guess the old retired professor in me would say I need to write the denouement to my life story." He stood up, groaned and stretched his back.

John stood and threw his arm over his brother's shoulder. "Don't know much about fancy literature words, but don't go thinking your story is wrapping up. They say seventy is the new fifty."

Samson couldn't muster a clever retort. He embraced his brother and, as he climbed into his rental car, said over his shoulder, "Say hi to Susan. Maybe I'll stop in on the way back."

As he pulled onto the freeway and headed west, he thought, 'for me, today, seventy feels like the new ninety.'

Samson drove under what the locals called a 'high sky'—cloudless, blue on the horizon but fading almost to white the higher your eyes drifted. He could see twenty miles in all directions. Even though this was the major roadway across the state, he drove for miles without seeing another vehicle. He stared at the concrete ribbon before him. *An ant… I'm nothing more than an ant crawling across an infinite, empty world. Are any of us ever anything more than that?*

As he exited the freeway, he saw a tractor pulling a baling machine gobbling up windrows of alfalfa and dropping huge cylinders of compacted hay on the pale green field. He replayed his memories of hauling hay with his dad and brother more than half a century ago. Hauling hay bales had been one of the few farm tasks they'd done together as a team. *What if I'd stayed home on the farm? Raised cattle, sold wheat…helped feed the world…Would I've felt better at seventy than I feel now?*

Shiny mirages of water danced on the state highway's black asphalt as he headed south. Fields on both sides of the road were green—sunflowers, soybeans, spring wheat. But their luster failed to penetrate the gray scrim that curtained Samson's thoughts. *I fed my family, that much I did…but what did I give this world? A couple of books full of stories…I suppose they gave some people a few minutes of distraction. Articles in literary journals read by other professors. And students….*

Samson slowed and turned right onto the gravel road for the last ten miles to the homestead. A sardonic smile crossed his face. *Ahh, students…I gave the world hundreds of*

As he approached the farmyard entrance, he noticed the old mailbox that had once stood alongside the road was gone. No people lived along this stretch of road. Farmsteads once occupied by houses, barns, gardens and families now held only grain storage bins and a few scraggly trees. Samson drove slowly up the narrow track to what was left of his childhood home. He stopped the car and stepped out into the immense silence of the Dakota spring, a silence so massive it seemed to thunder in his ears. He took a deep, painful breath and swept his eyes across the place. *The Stone House is long gone. The machine shed stood there. The old pig barn was there, alongside where the corral once was. The hay stacks were across that field, right next to where the chokecherries used to be—gone, all gone.*

Now, wherever he looked, he saw neat, endless rows of spring wheat, swaying in the perpetual breeze. The only interruption in this undulating ocean of green was the gravelly island inhabited by the gray, disintegrating building that Samson had once called home. He'd said a joyful good-bye to this place over half a century ago, come to terms with his parents' death decades ago. He had never seen himself as a nostalgic romantic. And yet, in an instant, he was overcome by a wave of grief so intense he leaned against the car and gulped down a sob. He hugged himself.

What am I mourning? The end of an era? Of Mom and Dad's story? Or the looming end of MY story? Damn, I should be grateful for all my years, for my family...That old Welsh poet said I should burn and rave and rage against the dying of the light. But here I stand...whimpering and sniveling.

Samson pushed himself erect, swiped his sleeve across his eyes and slowly walked toward the house. But that poem, the one he'd had hundreds of students parse over the years, continued to whisper in his thoughts. The second verse stopped him in his tracks.

'Though wise men at their end know dark is right, because their words had forked no lightning, they do not go gentle into that good night.'

Me? A wise man? I doubt it. And my words, all the millions of words that made up my life's work,…they've not set this world on fire, they've forked no lightning, that's for damn sure… But I'll go into my night like this house is soon going to go…with creaks and groans and a few sad puffs of dust.

Samson walked up the crumbing concrete steps to the back doorway. The frame of the screen door hung by one hinge, only a few tattered, rusting shreds of screen remained. He stepped across the inner door that lay sprawled across the entryway and walked into what had once been the kitchen. Spikes of glass were all that remained in the windows. Dust and dirt covered every surface and reduced the entering sunlight to a dull gray haze.

The walls were bare, no hints of the gallery of framed family photos his mother had once so eagerly assembled. All furnishings were gone, even the cupboards had been torn out. Then he shuffled into what had been the living room and there it sat. On the only stick of furniture in the entire house—a low, battered coffee table—sat the skull.

Samson was not shocked. He stood looking down. *Hello, old friend. What's it been—thirty years? Whoever broke the windows, stripped the walls and ransacked rooms probably didn't dare touch you. Maybe they thought you were cursed. Or maybe they looked into your eyes and you carried them somewhere they didn't want to go. No, I doubt it. Those who came to pillage and plunder didn't stop long enough for visions.*

Samson slowly lowered his aching joints to the dust covered floor. He knelt and picked up the skull, then leaned against the coffee table and set the skull in his lap. *I see you've lost some of your teeth..Yeah, we're all getting old. But the rest of you is still as I remember. And your eyes, ahhh, they're still deep and black and endless…*

*   *   *

"You gonna up and leave us jus' cuz of a dream?" Francis Chardon scratched his bald head in consternation. He wasn't happy with what one of his best workers had just told him.

Silas Howard, the tall, thin, sandy-haired forty-five-year-old, former barge hand, trapper and hunter, grinned down at the stocky director of the Fort Clark fur trading post. "Not just any dream, Francis. I've never had a dream like I had last night."

"Aww, you probly jus' had too much to drink."

Silas shooed the idea away with his hand "You know me. I can't stand whiskey. I had one beer with the boys before bed. No, this dream…I tell you, it was more like a vision…it was so… real."

"So… saw yer dead wife? Jus' a standin' at the foot of yer bed?"

"Minaki, my sunshine, there she was, and all around her there was this bright glow."

Francis returned to wiping down the counter of his store and shrugged. "Grief does strange things to a fella."

Silas' response was so unexpected, the director stopped his cleaning. The tall widower burst out laughing. "Francis, she died a year ago yesterday and I've done my share of grieving. But last night wasn't about grief. I'm telling you, she filled me with joy and anticipation."

Francis put down his rag and motioned for Silas to join him outside on a bench against the log walls of the stockade. The two men sat in the early morning July sunshine overlooking the prairie bluff that swept southward down to the Missouri. "All right, Silas, tell me again 'bout this vision and why ya think you gotta leave us."

*   *   *

In 1833, seven years before his dream vision, Silas Howard had caught his first glimpse of Fort Clark as he stood on the deck of a ship. He was part of the crew on the Assiniboine, one of the first steamboats to travel up the Big Muddy.

Silas was a bachelor who'd spent years hunting and trapping in the territory opened up by the great expedition of Lewis and Clark. Early in the spring of 1833 he hired on with the American Fur Company in St. Louis. He figured that after canoeing and poling his way upriver for years, being propelled by a paddlewheel would be a great diversion. He never expected the trip would change his entire life.

The journey began in St. Louis, in April, aboard the double-decked steamboat Yellow Stone. The ship's one hundred passengers waved and whooped to the crowds onshore as they headed upstream. Silas and the crew

71

had to constantly stoke the boiler whose steam kept the great engine pumping and the huge paddlewheel turning. Every evening, the boat pulled in to the riverbank. The Missouri's sandbars and underwater snags made nighttime travel a gamble the pilot refused to take. Besides this, the crew needed to go ashore to chop wood for the boiler and hunt game to feed the passengers.

Most of those aboard were employees of the American Fur Company, heading upriver to trap. But two of the men most definitely were not trappers. One morning, Silas had just finished his shift in the boiler room and came out on deck. The paddlewheel was churning through a smooth section of the river and the belching smoke was sweeping southward behind the boat. He noticed one of the well-dressed men standing near the railing and decided to introduce himself.

"Good morning, sir. I'm Silas Howard. I've notice noticed you often on deck."

"Good morning. Karl Bodmer is my name." The man's accent was strong. German, Silas thought.

The man smiled beneath his bushy moustache. "Yes, I come out here to work."

Silas was taken aback. *Is he serious or is he teasing me?*

Karl noted the deckhand's puzzled look and laughed. "My work is not with sweating like yours. I am employed as an artist."

"But you're not drawing or painting, I don't see any paper or brushes."

"Ah Herr Silas, the first work of the artist is not drawing, it is seeing." Karl pointed off to the right. "See how the water sweeps over that rock, how it shines white in the sunlight, how the ripples prance across the top. Before I can paint the water, I must see the water."

Silas gazed at the rock and his eyes were mesmerized. *The river is alive, it's dancing. I never knew…*

Karl spoke again, "Now, look there, on shore. See how the trees glow green like der smargard.. like, like the emerald in the light, but there, in the shadows, they are nearly black. An artist needs to learn how to look at the world. To see its wonders."

He put both hands on the rail and spoke more to himself than to Silas. "Most men go through life without truly seeing."

The men stood in the beauty of the morning, surrounded by the steady throbbing of the steam engine and the splashing of the huge paddlewheel. Silas couldn't help musing. *I've canoed this river, forded its tributaries, hunted and trapped along its banks, slept under the stars. But how much of my own life have I truly seen?*

Seven weeks later the Yellow Stone reached Fort Pierre and the passengers and crew transferred to her sister ship, the Assiniboine. Now they moved north and westward into Dakota Sioux territory. The crew was kept busy, poling the boat through shallows and even going ashore with ropes to pull it off of sandbars. One afternoon, Silas scrambled back aboard, soaked and muddy. He saw the artist Karl sitting on deck beside a man everyone on board knew simply as The Prince.

Silas began moving quietly past the pair when Karl called out, "Herr Silas, please to come here."

Silas approached and the men stood. Karl smiled, "I would like you to meet my employer, Prince Maximilian of Wied." Karl turned to the prince with a mischievous gleam in his eye, "This is Silas, one of our crew, the gentleman who is learning how to see the world."

Silas was embarrassed by the description and didn't know if he should bow or extend his muddy hand. The prince reached out, and with a firm grip and smile, eased the deckhand's uncertainty. "Good for you, Herr Silas. And thank you for your hard work. You are helping all of us see this great land."

The prince stood nearly as tall as Silas, and his face, unlike those of most of the crew and his hired artist, was clean shaven. He did have side whiskers that nearly reached his jawbone and wore a frock coat that, even after the long months aboard ship, looked surprisingly clean.

"Has Karl also taught you how to paint what you are seeing?"

Silas shook his head, "No sir, I'm afraid my hands are too rough to ever try anything like that."

The prince nodded and sat back down, "Well, maybe you should write down what you see. You could paint with words."

As the prince returned to his seat, Karl said, "Prince Maximillian has traveled to many lands and written books about his journeys."

Silas shrugged, "I've done my share of traveling and adventuring. I did learn my reading and writing, but I never had much time to do either one."

The prince said, "Well, our captain tells me that we will be spending our winter sheltered somewhere along this river until spring. You may have plenty of time to write or to paint."

Silas nodded. He was acquainted with Dakota winters. Everyone would have an abundance of time to fill. As he dismissed himself and moved on past the two men, he considered what he would do during the long cold months. What actually happened came as sheer surprise.

The boat made only a brief stop at Fort Clark that spring. Silas remembered how the trading post's vertical log walls stood in contrast to the dozens of rounded earthen lodges of the Mandan village that lay upstream from it. After only a day's rest, they moved onward.

At Fort Union, they left the paddle wheeler behind and boarded a sixty-foot keelboat. By the end of August, they had reached Fort Mckenzie,

American Fur Company's most remote wilderness. From the trading post's lookout, Silas could see the etchings of the mighty mountains, the ones the natives called the Rockies, lying like a blue dream on the far western horizon.

Two weeks later, Silas joined the small crew of oarsmen, and with Karl Bodmer and Prince Maximillian, began the thousand-mile journey back to Fort Clark. In early November, the boat rounded the bend and Silas spied the Mandan village and beyond it, Fort Clark. The icy fingers of winter already were hovering over the land. After months of intensive labor, Silas anticipated a season of rest. He did not foresee what this respite would bring.

*   *   *

Silas stood captivated. He'd never before observed an artist at work. Today Karl Bodmer had invited him into his makeshift studio inside Fort Clark as he worked on his latest portrait. Outside in the plaza, dogs barked and men bantered. But Silas heard nothing. He was fascinated by how confidently and quickly Karl could wield his water color brush and bring life to a sheet of paper stretched on his easel.

As Prince Maximillian had predicted, the days and weeks of the Dakota winter passed slowly. Silas had joined the Fort's team of hunters and several times a week went out to procure fresh meat. But that left many days unfilled. He often joined the other men in card games but since he was not a whiskey drinker, he seldom sat with them past midnight.

His favorite diversion was listening to the Prince tell of his travels to a place called Brazil. One day, Maximillian had shown him a copy of the book he'd written of that journey. Silas was fascinated by the stories of jungles with trees so high that bullets from the explorers' rifles could not reach the top branches and of brilliant green and blue parrots unafraid of humans.

Today was the first day Karl had allowed Silas watch him paint. For the first thirty minutes Silas's eyes were riveted to the artist's deft brushstrokes. Gradually he found himself drawn toward the Mandan woman whose portrait was being painted. She sat statue still, gazing at a point on the far wall. But unlike a statue she emanated a vibrant warmth, even in the chilly room. A few strands of her hair lay upon her shoulders but the rest stretched down her back. Scattered streaks of gray served to make the blackness of her hair more striking. She wore a deerskin shift, decorated with feathers. A half dozen necklaces of shells and beads curved around her long neck. Her lips were full, her mouth closed. The burnished red of her skin contrasted with the white of her deerskin dress. Silas was silently appreciating her quiet beauty when her obsidian eyes glanced toward him. Silas's eyes widened. *Did I see a smile on her face? Was she smiling at me?*

Minutes later he left the room, strangely unnerved by that fleeting smile. Though he'd had brief relationships with women in the past, he'd long ago convinced himself that bachelorhood was his destiny. But as he crunched through the snow to the Fort's store, the woman's smile hovered before his eyes. He entered the building and approached James Kipp, the store's clerk.

"Mr. Kipp, you speak Mandan don't you?"

"That I do, Mr. Howard. I had to learn it to court my wife."

Silas was intrigued, "You're married to a Mandan woman?"

Kipp laughed, "I'm not the only one. The winters are cold up here, the nights are long. And no white women have come this far north. We've been married for five years. We have a son, name of Samuel."

Silas paused, reluctant to continue. But that furtive smile…or was it seductive? "Kipp, that woman that Bodmer is painting today, do you know her?"

"The widow? Her name is Minaki, 'sunshine' in Mandan. Her husband was killed last year in a run-in with the Sioux. They'd been married four years, no children. She's returned to her parent's lodge. Easy on the eyes, isn't she?" The clerk cocked his head and smiled. "Getting ideas, eh, Silas? Well, she's a decent woman, quiet, seems to carry herself with pride."

Silas tried to shrug off Kipp's gentle teasing but that flustered attempt revealed he was indeed 'getting ideas,' though had anyone asked him what sort of ideas he was considering, he would have been flummoxed. As a trapper, he'd used castoreum, a pungent liquid made from a beaver's glands, mixed with cloves and cinnamon to attract a beaver to his trap. The animals, even knowing the dangers, could not resist the fragrances. That women's smile was an enticing attraction. Still, Silas might have resisted, had not Minaki made the next move.

As hard winter set in, the Mandan people left their lodges on the high bluff and moved down to their winter camp, to their smaller lodges sheltered among the trees along the banks of the Missouri. One evening James Kipp and his wife invited Silas to join them for a visit to the lower camp. They entered one of the lodges already crowded with people.

Kipp murmured into Silas's ear, "That old man in the center is the tribe's storyteller. He's retelling the Mandan creation story. Let's sit down here."

They quietly entered the circle and sat on the buffalo skins. Kipp began translating for Silas, as the animated speaker wove his tale. But Silas barely heard a word. No sooner had he sat down than Minaki had arisen from the other side of the lodge and settled by his side. Stunned, Silas looked down at her. She glanced up at him, gave him a gentle smile and leaned against his shoulder.

And so it began. In the weeks that followed, the bulwarks Silas had carefully constructed around his life were slowly dismantled. In the past he had shared his physical self with a woman, but he had never risked entrusting his emotional or spiritual being with another. Over the months of that winter, as he learned a few Mandan words and Minaki learned some English, Silas made an extraordinary discovery. For most of his adult life, without realizing it, he had been lonely. He'd simply assumed the hollow space within his heart was common to all humanity. When Minaki's warm love finally flooded into his life, and when he gave himself completely to her, he was finally able to identify the condition of loneliness that he'd thought was a normal part of being a man.

*   *   *

In mid-April of 1834, when the freshly caulked keel boat set off on its journey back to St. Louis, Silas stood on the riverbank with his wife Minaki and waved farewell to the artist and the prince and the crew. In the three years that followed he learned how to be a husband. Thanks to James Kipp, he learned more of the Mandan language. And thanks to Minaki, he grew in his understanding of a woman's unique communication.

The couple occupied the small shelter alongside the fort that had been hastily constructed as the winter home for the artist and the prince, though they often spent time in the earthen lodge of Minaki's family. Silas continued his work as one of the Fort's hunters, while Minaki joined the rest of the Mandan women tending the fields of corn, pumpkins, squash and beans.

Not since his youth had Silas dwelt so long in one place. For nearly two decades he'd been driven to seek the best hunting grounds, the ideal trapping territory; always on the move, never content. But now, thanks to Minaki, Silas began savoring their settled life, the daily routines, their shared laughter as they tried to learn each other's language. In the shelter of her embrace, Silas found a home.

In 1837, his home was devastated. That spring, the American Fur Company's steamboat, on the journey upriver, made its annual stop at Fort Clark. As usual, all of the inhabitants of the Fort and the Mandan village greeted the boat's arrival and welcomed the crew ashore. The steamboat stayed only one night. When it departed the next morning, it left behind a horrific invader.

A week after the boat left, several people in the village developed fevers. Within days, dozens of men, women and children were burning with high temperatures. When rashes appeared, Silas desperately tried to keep Minaki away from the village.

He gripped her shoulders, "Sunshine, this is the pox. If it attacks you, you'll die."

Minaki looked up at him, sighed and granted him a resigned smile, "Husband, this is my family. I must.." she searched for words, "give them care. I cannot hide."

Silas released her, sadly admitting it was her caring, her outpouring nature that had conquered his own heart. How could he prevent her from being herself?

Minaki spent the next weeks rubbing salves on blistered scabs, soothing fevered brows with soaking rags. When he wasn't out hunting, Silas worked alongside her. But one by one, the people died. The old, the young—all covered with pustules, burning with fever, dying in agony. At first, the survivors tried to honor the dead in the customary way, wrapping the dead in buffalo robes and lifting them to scaffolds on the prairie. Silas helped lift more than one body up to its airy resting place. But soon, the bodies were too many, and the men too few. Eventually, the dead were laid to rest in hastily dug shallow graves.

*   *   *

It was July, and in the nearly deserted village, the sound of whimpers were a counterpoint to the buzzing of the flies. The malevolent marauder had finally attacked Minaki. Months ago, Silas had resigned himself to this moment. Though he'd never been a religious man, he'd whispered and shouted words to the God his parents worshipped and to Manitou, the Great Spirit of Minaki's people. He'd spoken endless words of love to Minaki. But now his supply of words was exhausted. He could only soothe her brow with a damp cloth. His low keening attended her last lingering gasps, then she was gone. His Sunshine had departed. He was bereft.

For months he stumbled through the daylight hours like a blinded ghost. His nights were haunted by specters of the dead and fleeting glimpses of his dying wife. Nine out of every ten members of the tribe had perished. The haggard remnant looked with deep suspicion upon the white men who had gone untouched by the plague. Even those few members of Minaki's family who had survived now regarded Silas with distrust.

The winter that followed was brutal. As the snow piled up higher, the temperature plummeted lower. Ironically, it was the harshness of the weather that pulled Silas out of his paralyzing despair. The Fort's residents and the meager population of the Mandan village needed food. Silas and a few other men had to venture out farther and farther to find game. The arduous effort to feed others brought Silas back from darkest despair. Deep grieving eased, and slowly he was able to resume some semblance of life as part of the Fort

Clark family. However, the colors of his world were now muted and dull. He came to accept the dim despondency of his life as the price he'd paid for finding love.   Until last night, when Minaki came to him in a dream…

*   *   *

Francis Chardon, the Fort Clark director sighed, "All right, Silas, tell me again about this vision and why ya think you gotta leave us."

Silas wished James Kipp still ran Fort Clark. He would have understood Silas's explanation. But Kipp had gone west two years ago. Mr. Chadron did not speak Mandan and distrusted those who did. Silas scrambled for words.

"Middle of the night…I heard my name. I opened my eyes and there she was, my wife, Minaki, smiling, surrounded by light. Right there at the foot of my bed. I started to speak but she held up her hand…it glowed in the dark. She said, 'Time's current is swift. You must live. Live my Silas.'"

The skeptical director shrugged, "Nothin' new there. Time passes and you're livin' just as much as the rest of us, I'd say."

Silas ignored Francis's comment and continued, "Then she said, 'Go, my dear heart, venture south, see like the artist, weave words like the prince. Live, Silas, live. Our spirits will meet again on the plains.'" Silas's eyes shone as he savored her words.

Francis shook his head, "This all just sounds like fever talk to me. Ya sure you're not sick?"

Silas leaned back against the log walls of the fort and let his eyes drift to the feathery clouds above. *I suppose I could try to explain…tell him about Karl and Prince Maximillian…about the ways they painted the world with color and words and how Minaki and I found love during their time with us…But…hell, time's current is swift.*

"I'm not sick, no fever." Silas leaned forward, put his hands on his knees and quickly stood, "I'm leaving Fort Clark today. Gonna take me a summer time meander on the prairie."

Francis rolled his eyes and stood looking up at the grizzled widower. "Sound's crazy to me, but you're a free man. I suppose you'll be wantin' a horse."

Silas shook his head, "Naw. One man on a horse might be too tempting for the Sioux. But I think I'll take that mutt, Rufus for company. I'll travel light. Still, I'll be needing some supplies. I'll get my bedroll and my pack and meet you at the store."

Francis watched in bewilderment as Silas exuberantly bounded toward the barracks.

*   *   *

Summer's nighttime cloak lay gently over the prairie. The red-haired dog laid his long jaw on his paws and whined.

"What's the matter, Rufus? Afraid of the dark?" Silas pulled his hand out from under the blanket and ruffled the scraggly hair on the dog's head. They'd left around noon and ambled about ten miles south of the Fort. Silas had shot a jack rabbit for supper. Rufus had dined on the entrails and then sniffed around the clearing in the chokecherry trees where they'd set up camp. The dog had grown up inside the confines of the fort and now seemed perplexed.

Silas pulled the dog closer to his bedroll, "Don't worry, boy. Dogs and men can survive outside of walls. I did it for years. Maybe we both need to relearn that skill." Rufus lifted his head, stared into Silas's eyes, then sighed, dropped his jaw onto his paws and fell asleep.

Seven hours later, they were awakened by the high-pitched whistling of the hundreds of sparrows who roosted in the chokecherry trees around the camp. Only the faintest promise of dawn tinged the eastern horizon but the birds were already heralding the new day. Silas put his hands behind his head and looked up into the rosy purple sky. *Just like my Minaki…early risers, full of joy.* He stretched and sat up and the dog followed suit.

As Silas boiled water for his coffee he mused, "What wonders will we see today, Rufus? I've spent most of my time on the plains looking for something to hunt or trap. Lots of looking, not much seeing. Let's make today different."

The man and his dog headed south toward a low range of hills. The prairie grass, pale green only months ago, was now dried to a tawny brown. They reached the crest of the hill and a rolling plain lay before them. A cloud of dust moved toward them from the east.

"Sit down, ol' Rufus. There's an impressive parade a'coming." As a hunter, Silas had stalked buffalo, hunted and killed buffalo. Today he anticipated the chance to simply watch the magnificent beasts. A herd of hundreds was plodding westward, their sharp hooves stirring up the dry soil. In the center of the mass, the calves born in March trotted alongside the cows. On the margins, plodded the shaggy, horned and humped bulls. Silas could feel the deep vibration of the ground beneath them. Even Rufus sensed it and whined as he fixed his eyes on the approaching herd. Calves bleated for their mothers, the cows grunted and the bulls emitted resonant rumblings from deep within their massive chests.

The herd now was moving past them, a hundred yards away on the plain below. Rufus could not contain himself. He leapt to all fours and began barking. His yaps were nearly swallowed up by the noise of the moving bison. But one mountainous bull stopped his march and turned his beady eyes toward them. Silas knew these beasts were near-sighted, but their sense of hearing and smell were keen. He tried to grab the yelping Rufus. The bull's tail went up, the beast snorted once, twice, then bellowed. Apparently, Rufus realized his imprudence. Not only did he stop barking, he flattened himself onto the prairie and began to whimper. Silas held his breath. At last the great bull shook his shaggy head and resumed his duty as protector of the moving herd.

Silas lay his hand on the dog's head. "Boy, you can't go challenging a beast like that. One thing we need to remember out here on the prairie. Most of the time, we aren't the ones running the show. Buffalo and blizzards, storms and snakes—they all remind us we're not in control. We gotta stay humble, Rufus." As Silas stroked the dog's back, he remembered his own futility as the voracious pox consumed the Mandan, one by one, until it devoured Minaki. *Humility…if we don't learn it, life will crush us.*

During the last week of August, the man and his dog meandered over the endless prairie. Since in Silas's dream-vision Minaki had said 'go south', they generally moved in that direction, allowing the valleys and ridges to shape their route. One sun drenched morning, as Rufus scooted after a rabbit, Silas broke off his tuneless whistling and filled his lungs with the dry, clean air. In the azure sky, white cloudships sailed along in the breeze. Far to the west, two mesas carved notches in the blue sky. Low rolling hills fell off to the east. To the north behind him, and the south before him, the horizon stretched to infinity. *I'm a trifling speck on this great plain.* He laughed out loud. *What a great relief. No burdens to carry. My living and my dying—sure, they're precious to me, but this world will do just fine, with or without me.* He grinned as a panting Rufus came back to his side. "Well, I suppose you'd still need a little tending if I was gone, wouldn't you, boy?" The dog's tail wagged in agreement as they ambled into the golden August day.

That evening, they reached the river. The sun had just set. In the mauve evening air, the nighthawks hovered, then dove down after insects, emitting a low wooop at the bottom of each dive. Silas and Rufus stood on a bluff looking down on the water that glinted in the sun's afterglow.

Silas murmured, "Looks like we've reached the Heart River. Minaki called it the Ches-Che-Tar. She never told me what that meant. I'll stick with 'Heart.'" He stared down into the slow current as a wave of melancholy and loss swept over him. Rufus's barking brought him back to the moment. The dog had wandered downstream and up into a small hollow. Silas followed the sound of his yapping. The dog stood before what looked like the remains of a log shack partially set inside the hill.

"Calm down boy. I don't think you'll roust anyone out of this old cabin. Looks like what's left of an old trapper's shelter." The walls were mostly intact, but only part of the roof remained. There was no door and when Silas peered into the dusky interior, he heard the scurrying of small paws. "Come away, Rufus. Appears as though this room is already occupied. We'll see what it looks like in the daylight."

Over the next few days Silas cleaned out the little cabin and used some fallen branches to make a crude door. Enough of the roof remained so he could have a fairly dry corner if it should rain. He decided he would stay here for the next weeks. In his dream vision, his Sunshine had whispered of the meeting of their spirits.

Something about this place—the quiet current, the tawny hillsides, the chill evening air—soothed his soul and made that encounter seem possible. He planned on staying here until winter drove him back to Fort Clark. Like many of life's plans, that was not to be.

*   *   *

Silas was on his knees digging up a few wild onions he planned on using to season the venison stew he was going to make for supper. His deerskin bag already had a half dozen prairie turnips he'd dug up earlier. Minaki had taught him where to look for these tubers. They'd be a good addition to the meal. He sat back on his haunches and wiped sweat from his brow. His damp shirt clung to his back. The heavy air had cast a gauzy film over the sun. A day ago, the usual prevailing northwesterly breeze had swung around to the southeast. Now, under the midafternoon's hazy glare, that breeze died completely and an ominous stillness settled over the prairie—no meadowlark trillings, no locust chirrings—only a heavy silence. Silas stood, shaded his eyes and studied the western horizon. A rippling line of gray, innocent appearing clouds arced from north to south.

Silas had lived long enough on the plains to read the signs. He murmured as he walked toward the ramshackle cabin, "Mother Nature's preparing one of her spectaculars. I've had to outrun storms, hide from storms, save boats and beasts from storms. Today I'm gonna sit and observe this performance."

He dropped his bag of onions and turnips inside the shack, brought his pack inside and made sure his bedroll was in the driest corner. Then he hiked to the top of the hill. Rufus plodded beside him. The dog's tail, usually wagging, hung low and still. Silas climbed onto a sun-warmed boulder and lifted the dog up to join him. "You can feel the storm coming too, can't you boy? I don't know how long you'll want to stay up here with me. It's gonna get wild."

Gradually, the gray clouds on the distant horizon coalesced. Then, over the next hour, the mass began to bubble up, a thick froth of white against the hazy blue sky. Silas wondered how the prince who painted with words would have described it. *Like mushrooms growing on top of mushrooms, white smoke pouring from the steamship's stacks.* What had been a line of clouds on the horizon, was now a stately mountain range, marching across the prairie. The towering cloud peaks continued to surge upward, roiling, folding, enfolding.

Silas looked up as sunlight dimmed. He sat surrounded by a leaden stillness. But high above, a ravenous wind ripped ragged clots from the towering cloud peaks. These now streamed ahead of the mountainous masses and blotted out the sun. The white mushroom clouds were now heavy, bruise-purple clusters flashing and flaring with internal fire. Beneath the mass was an ominous band of darkness, riven over and over again by spears of forked lightning. Rufus began to whine.

"Fearsome isn't it, boy. But awesome too. A sky creature come to life, rampaging across the land." Now they began to hear rumblings, faint grinding noises, like rocks tumbling over each other. The sound grew until it reminded Silas of barrels tumbling down stairs. Then from the heart of the blackness, a bolt shot out and struck the hilltop miles upriver and within seconds the thunderclap echoed across the plain. A gray veil dropped from the cloud and began advancing toward them. Icy whirlpools of wind swirled the grass around their boulder. Rufus was crying now and Silas hopped down and grabbed the dog.

"C'mon ol' Rufus, let's run and see if we can beat the rain."

They were halfway down the hill when the first huge drops splashed upon them. "Oooeee! That's cold!" Silas shouted joyfully. Man and dog were soaked and panting by the time they reached the little cabin. The wind driven rain pelted down for twenty minutes as Silas and Rufus huddled in the corner. Continuous growling thunder and bursts of lightning kept the poor dog trembling. Silas consoled him. "Mother Nature's not after you, boy. Don't take it personal. She's just blowing off some steam, reminding us who is in charge of this land."

The rumbling gradually faded as the storm hurried across the plain. When the rain stopped, they stepped around the puddles on their cabin floor and emerged into a freshly washed world. The storm's backside was a deep purple wall to their east. It wore a faint rainbow, painted there by the last rays of the setting sun. Silas had saved enough dry wood to start a cooking fire. By the time the evening star appeared and the bullfrogs and crickets began their nighttime serenades, the venison stew was ready to eat.

*   *   *

In mid-September, the first frost visited the Heart River plains. Silas and Rufus emerged from their cabin and blinked as the sun's first rays glinted on the snowy sheen that coated the grass. Within hours the frost had disappeared and the day warmed. The next weeks were full of summery sunshine. Silas remembered Minaki and her family describing the balmy days that always seemed to follow the first frost. The men at the fort simply referred to it as "Indian summer." The nights were often chilly but the days were pleasant. The leaves on the few trees and bushes along the river exchanged greens for yellows and reds. Silas began to contemplate his return to the fort. But one morning in mid-October changed everything.

Silas was awakened by a low growl. Early morning light filtered through the chinks in the walls. Rufus stood with his nose pressed against the rough cabin door, a deep rumbling in his throat. "What's going on boy? Something out there?"

Silas grabbed the scruff on his dog's neck and opened the door. Only twenty feet away, at the edge of the clearing, stood a coyote. Its head was lowered, yet it seemed to glare balefully at the man and the dog. *Why would a coyote, the shyest of critters, stand here in the morning light and not run away?* In the same instant that the answer flashed into Silas's mind, Rufus tore away from Silas's grip and flew toward the gray animal.

"No, Rufus, no," Silas screamed as he raced after his dog. But the two beasts were already a rolling, snarling blur of red and gray fur. As Silas drew near, he could see the slavering foam in the mouth of the diseased coyote. He grabbed one of Rufus's hind legs and tried to pull him away but the dog's jaws were clamped on the coyote's hindquarters. When Silas jerked, both animals tumbled toward him in a ball. The slathering, bloody mass rolled over him. He jumped to his feet and sprinted to the cabin for his gun. When he emerged, Rufus and the coyote were a yard apart. The afflicted animal tottered drunkenly with its jaws wide open. Rufus readied himself to lunge once more. Silas raised his rifle and shot. The coyote yelped once and dropped. Rufus jumped back at the gunshot but then began to limp toward the carcass.

"No, Rufus, stop. Come here." Silas ran and grabbed his bloodied, filthy dog. "Oh Rufus, Rufus, what have you done?" Tears filled Silas's eyes as he examined the wounds on his friend's body. The white of bone shone through a deep gash on one leg. A flap of flesh hung down from the dog's lip. A bloody tear angled across his chest. The wounds were serious, but not fatal. Given enough time, they would heal. But Silas sadly shook his head. In all probability, Rufus would not have that much time.

Silas carried the dog to a spot beside the cabin door. He fetched river water and washed out the wounds as best he could. Then he took a rawhide cord, wrapped it around the dead coyote's leg and dragged the already stiffening body downstream and tossed it into the water. As he trudged back to the cabin, he pulled off his torn and bloody shirt. Beneath the dirt on his right arm was a three-inch scratch. He stopped in his tracks and stared at the innocuous scrape. Decades ago, he'd seen his hunting partner Jonas succumb to hydrophobia. Jonas had been bitten by a racoon and two weeks later, was beset with fever and vomiting. Within days his muscles grew weak, he began raving and had a delirious fear of water. His death had not been easy.

Silas returned to the cabin. Rufus's tail happily thumped the ground as his master sat down on the dirt beside him. "Rufus, looks like we've run into one of nature's calamities. That critter was sick. Whoever saw a coyote standing like that, stock still in broad daylight?…And if he was afflicted by hydrophobia… well, our chances aren't too good. But don't worry, boy. I'll see to you, one way or another. We'll know, sooner or later."

During the week that followed, when Silas went out hunting, he had to tie up Rufus so he would not try to follow. He made a bed of grass for the dog outside the cabin and several times a day rubbed bear grease on the dog's wounds. They appeared to be healing. But on the eighth day after the attack, Rufus would not eat and when Silas set down a bowl of water, the dog edged backward. The next morning, when Silas reached down to pet him, Rufus bared his teeth and snarled. Silas jumped back and shook his head. "I know that's not you, boy, it's the sickness. Won't get any better, I'm afraid."

Silas spent most of the day watching his dog and trying to prepare himself for what he needed to do. Gray clouds blanketed the sky and a blustery northwesterly wind promised rain. It was late afternoon, about an hour before sunset when Silas loaded his rifle. Rufus shivered but did not move when Silas approached.

"Rufus, you've been a good dog, a good friend. I'm doing you a kindness." He pulled the trigger, the dog barely moved. The shot echoed against the bluffs across the Heart.

The next day, under gray drizzling skies, Silas used his hunting knife to dig a hole in the dirt beneath some juneberry shrubs. The soil there was softer than the prairie sod, but nonetheless he was sweating by the time he had a hole big enough to bury Rufus. Afterward, he sat in the dim cabin, listening to the rain's dismal dripping. Rufus's absence filled the room. Silas was sad, but not glum. *Minaki's message to me was so true: 'time's current is swift'. Like so many of her people, she was swept away. Wonder how soon I'll join her? Joining her…that thought's appealing. Getting from here to there…can't say I'm looking forward to that.* The images of his old hunting partner Jonas's painful death swirled into his mind. Then with a start he jumped up, moved to the doorway and stood gazing out toward the mist laden river. *Wait, no, I won't waste whatever time I have looking forward. Minaki told me to live now, told me our spirits would meet out here on the plains. I'll see what the world still has to offer me, savor every sight like it was a mouthful of my venison stew.* He turned away from the door, got out his kettle, and began preparing supper for one.

*   *   *

In the fading sunlight, Silas plodded up the slope of the tallest bluff alongside the river. Four days ago, he'd buried Rufus. Today, his throat began to itch and he felt as though a fire smoldered in each of his joints. He knew the hike upward would exhaust him, but he was bent on reaching the top before sunset. He wasn't sure of the day's number on the calendar. He wasn't sure if it was the end of October or the beginning of November. But he'd sojourned long enough out on these plains to know that tonight he would be treated to the rising of what Minaki's people called the Hunter's Moon. For the Mandan and the Sioux of the high plains, this full moon signaled the start of the fall hunt. The animals had fattened themselves in preparation for the approaching winter and the hunters needed to harvest enough of them so they and their families could survive the months of ice and snow.

Deep within his mind, Silas knew he would not survive those months. But tonight, he refused to allow that thought to hinder his climb. He struggled upward, gasping and sweating in the chill evening air. He reached the crest and sunk gratefully down beside a buff-colored sandstone boulder, just in time for the spectacle.

On the western horizon, the sun slowly sank. At the same time, at the eastern rim of the prairie, the moon gradually emerged—a great, orange lustrous ball. The entire landscape was bathed in the merging light of setting sun and rising moon, a pale purple luminescence. Silas sat, awed by the beauty of the scene and replayed memories of his many hunts—the scouting, stalking, and silent waiting for animals to pass near. Unconsciously he slipped into what he thought of as his 'stillness'. As he leaned against the boulder, he slowed his breathing, allowed his muscles to relax, and sought to become one with the earth and rock.

Silas was staring unblinking out into the night as the moon steadily rose, it's orange transforming into pearly white. Then a shadow passed between him and the moon, and he sensed a presence on the boulder. He managed not to flinch but he did roll his eyes to the left and up. *My God, a snowy owl. Never saw one in the fall, never so close...* His heart leapt, but he willed himself to calm his breathing. Only an arm's length away, the two-foot-tall bird sat statue still, staring out over the vast prairie. Silas closed his eyes, reached out his mind, and caught a glimpse of the world through the great owl's eyes: sunlight glinting on ice-glazed snow, jackrabbits zig-zagging across open grasslands, lofty swoops and screeching dives.

Ten minutes later, as silently as it arrived, the great owl swooped out into the night. Silas felt a great soaring freedom as he watched it disappear. *Was this a sign? No doubt it means winter is coming soon. But was there something more in its visitation?* He pulled himself up and gingerly picked his way down the hill. The smoldering pain in his joints was invading his body, but a quiet calm was blossoming in his heart. *Soon, soon I will be soaring above the pain.*

The next morning, Silas did not arise from his buffalo robe blanket. Fever rolled over him in waves. Toward evening he opened bleary eyes and stared up as a fine powdering of snow drifted through the cracks in the ceiling. He groaned and pulled the robe over his head. A banshee wind began howling from the northwest and rattled the branches of the crude door.

The blizzard continued through the night. And somewhere within the turmoil of fevered dreams and delirious visions Silas saw the next step on his journey. Whether it was a hallucination or a moment of lucid insight, he could not discern. He was beyond all discerning. He stood, wrapped the robe around his shivering, fiery body and pulled open the door. Dawn had come an hour ago, but in the raging wind and pelting snow, visibility was only a few feet. But Silas did not need to see far. He knew where he was going. Twenty feet ahead was the bank of the river. There, the prairie stopped abruptly and fell ten feet to a narrow beach lapped by the Heart. Silas knew that the wind-driven snow would sail over this edge and drop into a huge drift against this bank.

The wind pummeled his back and hastened his steps toward the river. He stood for a second on the precipice, then let himself fall. Several feet of snow cushioned his arrival. He rewrapped his robe, lay down parallel to the river, and waited for the blizzard to complete his tomb. The snow cooled his face. He smiled as he thought of the great spirit soaring in a creamy white sky.

*   *   *

The Mandan peoples believed the frail crocus flower had a special power. The song of the crocus encourages all other plants to awaken.

The winter had been harsh and long. Blizzard after blizzard had pounded the plains, followed by Arctic blasts so brutal that many animals died. Slowly, as March surrendered to April, the snow began to melt. Now, only patches of icy crust remained on the open plain pierced by the light purple blooms of the crocuses.

The ramshackle trapper's cabin had collapsed under the winter's heavy snows and now was but a heap of logs in the melting slush. Twenty feet to the south, were the banks of the Heart and below them the ten-foot snow drifts slumped in the warming sun. The rising waters quickly eroded the icy crystals and revealed a buffalo robed body.

As the swirling current consumed the last of the snow, the body of Silas Howard slid into the bosom of the river and disappeared.

*   *   *

The sound of the gurgling flood still lingered in Samson Bartz's ears as he slowly opened his eyes. The skull lay on his lap, so placid and passive, no hint of its mysterious capacity. A cranium found lodged in the banks of the river, nothing more. And yet...

Samson sat on the dusty floor trying to recover his temporal balance. *The year is 2018, I'm seventy years old, the month is June...* He blinked in the dim light and relocated himself...*I'm a retired, lonely old man and I'm sitting in the sad remnants of what was once my home.* But the glum awareness of who and where he was now competed with the dramatic images and events of the life he'd witnessed through this time-leaping skull...steamboats, artists and princes, love and loss, snowy owls and storms, dying and living...*Why did this drama come to me? Does it have a meaning? Is it meant to be a message?*

His head throbbed and a spasm of nausea gripped his stomach. He feared he would be sick. He forced himself to take slow, deep breaths. Gradually he reestablished his equilibrium. As he calmed himself, long submerged remembrances bobbed to the surface of his consciousness. *I was almost twelve... in the attic... the feeling I had the first time I stared into those eyes...When I came back from the Sioux...ohhh..there was confusion, oh yes...but more...a delicious sense that I had a secret...a secret that gave me power and courage. And then...decades ago. How old was I in that summer of our disconnect? I came back from the trappers' story gasping...gasping in fear, staggered by my myopic view of our life together...that story..that vision...it saved our marriage...*

He sat for five minutes replaying those past emotions, then thought perhaps he should stand. But his old bones were not yet ready and so, though his latest sojourn was still overwhelming and vivid, he tentatively began probing how it might be altering his soul. Images and words whirled: *Sunshine, snow owls, live, see, weave with words, savor...* He allowed the mysterious story to bathe his mind. He sensed a softening of the brittle shell he'd been wearing for months. *Can this vision give anything to my worn-out life? Dispel any of its drab grayness?*

At last, with a grunt he grabbed hold of the table and levered himself up. He picked up the skull, cradled it in the crook of his arm and stepped out of the house's dimness onto the crumbling cement steps. He blinked as his eyes accommodated to the flashing mid-afternoon sun. He made a decisive resolution: he turned his back on the derelict, lifeless building. *I will no longer lament for this jumble of boards and dry wall.* His next move was made not by a conscious resolve, but was triggered more by instinct than decision. By an inherent compulsion almost seven decades old, he began moving toward the Heart River.

He walked along the narrow strip of grass that lay between the wheat fields. On the path ahead of him, a killdeer began squawking through the grass. She stayed only a few feet ahead of him, dragging a wing and appearing to hobble on one of her stilt-like legs. The desperate female, by pretending to be injured and easy prey, was attempting to lead him away from the fledglings in her nest. Samson grinned at her ruse "Ah momma bird, don't worry. I'm no threat to you and your little ones. Soon your babies will fly. As Dad always said, 'Live and let live'."

After leading him on for twenty feet, the bird sprung into the sky with a victorious cry, 'kill-dee, kill-dee.' The breeze rippled through the grain field, sending shimmers of green toward him. Samson's feet carried him forward as he mused. *Live...I thought I was writing my denouement. But is there more for me to live? More story for me to write? More chapters to my life?*

The wheat fields ended fifty feet from the river. The short grass still held its springtime green and clumps of blooming pink prairie roses dotted the plain. He didn't notice them until he stepped directly on one plant. Samson quietly rebuked himself. *The roses...jeez, now I'm trampling on the roses.* He recalled how he'd pricked his fingers picking a bouquet for his mother when he was a boy. He'd brought her roses, bluebells, crocuses. Those who hurried across this land never saw them. But the prairie held flowers and because they were scattered and sparse, they were precious.

He reached the edge of the bluff and stood looking down at the river twenty feet below. The water looked dark and cool, the current still steady from the spring rains. He followed the crest until it dipped down into a coulee that led out onto a grassy meadow edged by juneberry bushes. A wide flat limestone rock lay next to the water. Samson sat down and placed the skull on the rock beside him.

This particular rock was an old friend. As a boy he'd stood here fishing, hoping for lunkers, but mostly catching six-inch bullheads. As a young teen he'd flopped down on this yellow-gray bench, stared into the sky, imagining the journeys and adventures he would have. Later, he'd discovered science fiction novels and been intrigued by time travel and time machines that could send you into the future. That future was always full of marvels: flying cars, floating cities, exotic alien life forms. That adolescent fascination led him to write his PhD dissertation on time travel. Since that writing he'd only managed to travel four and a half decades forward in time. Now, as the summer air began to cool along the riverbank, he looked down at the skull resting beside him.

Not a shiny time machine, just an old brainpan belonging to...God only knows. And yet somehow...a time traveling device that three times has taken me backward, not forward in time. And it didn't exactly carry me into the past, not me as Samson Bartz...I wasn't like the Connecticut Yankee in King Arthur's Court that Mark Twain imagined. No...this time traversing skull transported me into the life of another—a young Sioux, a beleaguered trapper, a wandering hunter.

He looked out over the water. The ripples still clung to a few rays of the sunshine's gold. *All times are somewhere in the river—upstream, downstream. And we.. we carry the stories of those times within us. The stories of this place flow in and through our lives. Submerged, usually, but still present. The native peoples, the explorers, hunters and settlers…and the land too—the coulees and creeks, buttes and prairies—they all carry the tales that quietly, covertly shape our lives. My hero, Ursula LeGuin, the great time travel writer said, 'Other people's stories may become part of your own, the foundation of it, the ground it goes on.'*

He smiled to himself as he remembered one summer when he was ten. He and Johnny, while exploring the old gravel pit, found an arrowhead. As he held it in his palm, he imagined the hands that made it, the arms that stretched the bow and sent the arrow flying, the thundering heart of the beast it felled. All of that, the spirit of it all, dwelt in that bit of carved flint. He silently nodded at a new insight.

We're always time traveling. We're always shaping and reshaping the past, thinking and rethinking future. 'The thing about working with time, instead of against it, is that it is not wasted. Even pain counts.' *Ursula said that too.* 'Even pain counts'*…I remember reading and rereading that line, trying to decipher her meaning.*

A flock of mourning doves settled into trees across the river and began their sad five toned lament. Their melancholy air swept over Samson and he realized that as a young man, he'd been stymied in his attempt to understand that phrase because his notion of pain had been abstract. He'd been too naïve, too sheltered. He hadn't known the stab of deep, dreadful pain. But now, having lived through the trauma of his oldest son's addiction, the harrowing struggle to restore and rebuild his marriage, the shock of a colleague's suicide, and now Diane's Alzheimers…now he understood more of pain. As the doves continued their keening, a phrase from his very first skull vision surfaced, words spoken in an ancient voice.

'Breaking is part of living, a sharpening to make us more useful.'

Breaking…I've endured my share of that lately…But sharpened? Made more useful? If anything, I've lost my usefulness. Diane doesn't need me, my kids don't need me, the university doesn't need me…

He was beginning to feel that heavy blanket of sadness settle upon him when a dark shape burst from the water and flopped down with a great splash. Within seconds a second fish flew a foot into the air and smacked onto the water, then another and another. Each fish was at least three feet long. After a minute the spectacle subsided and the river's surface calmed.

He chuckled, *Carp jumping, I haven't seen that in ages, not since we were kids. They sure set the water a churning. Wait'll I tell Johnny.*

As he considered the words and metaphors he would use to describe the event, it struck him. *That's what I do. What I've always done. I tell stories. Before I was a professor, or a husband, or a father...I was a storyteller. Maybe that's why I'm still here. To see with the eye of the artist, to speak and write with the storyteller's flair. Maybe I'm still around so I can help keep imagination alive. To tell tales that stir minds, set hearts racing, write stories that delight. I'm still breathing, I'm still alive...I can still wait for snow owls and savor hunter's moons.*

My dear Diane...she may forget my face, forget me...I'll need to bear that pain. But I can still tell stories, for her, and the others who surround her there. My grandchildren, so busy and distracted...still, maybe, perhaps, I could write stories to delight them... And, why not..I could write a time travel story about a boy, a river, and a mystical skull.

He pulled in his legs, knelt, then picked up the skull.

Now what am I going to do with you? You're not mine. No doubt you belong to the first person who inhabited you, but now, somehow, you hold the stories of this river and this land.

Still clutching the skull, Samson awkwardly stood up and faced the water. *Who can tell who next may need your tales of courage and insight? That is not for me to say. I will let the Heart decide.*

Samson held the skull like a bowling ball, pulled back his arm and then swung it forward. The skull flew upward. The river was all in shadow but at the peak of its arc the skull flashed white in the last rays of the setting sun. Then it tumbled downward into the purpling dusk and splashed into the waters.

The doves had ceased their mourning, the only sound was the river's gentle murmuring. The old man stood for a moment, then turned and began his journey home.

AUTHOR'S NOTES

The seed that sprouted this story: The farmstead where I grew up still exists in southwestern North Dakota. It lies on the banks of Antelope Creek, a tributary of the Heart River. In the 1930's, when my father was a boy, his older brother found a skull embedded in the bank of that creek. When I was a boy in the 1950's, I saw and held that skull. My little brother and I never thought of it as macabre or frightening. I left the farm in the late 60's. Though the farmhouse, and some of the outbuildings still stand, the whereabouts of the skull is unknown.

The people who populate this story: This entire story is a work of fiction and most of its characters are products of my imagination. Here are a few exceptions:

The names of the two trappers in part two are taken from records of the Lewis and Clark Expedition. Only a few facts are known about either one. My story of their adventure on the Heart River is fictional.

Peter Weiser was born and reared Pennsylvania. He was active in the fur trade after the Expedition and traveled widely across the northwest. In an 1810 manuscript map, Clark shows a Weiser River, a tributary of the Snake River in western Idaho. In Clark's 1825-1828 "List of Men on Lewis and Clark's Trip," Weiser is listed as "killed." **https://www.pbs.org/lewisandclark/inside/pweis.ht ml**

John B. Thompson's date and place of birth are not known. He may have lived in Indiana Territory, and may have had some surveying experience. During the Expedition Clark praised him as "a valuable member of our party." In Clark's 1825-1828 "List of Men on Lewis and Clark's Trip," Thompson is listed as "killed."
https://www.pbs.org/lewisandclark/inside/jthom.html

Rene Jusseaume or Jessaume, was a free trader who, in 1804, had already lived with the Mandans for about fifteen years. He acted as Mandan interpreter for many persons, but apparently was not considered a good one. He participated fully in the social and ceremonial life of the Mandans, which may account for some of the low opinions held by many whites. Alexander Henry the Younger called him "that old sneaking cheat."
https://lewisandclarkjournals.unl.edu/item/lc.jrn.1804-10-27#lc.jrn.1804-10-27.01

Big White or Sheheke was the main civil chief at Mitutanka, the Mandan village at the time of the arrival of Merriweather Lewis and William Clark among the Mandan in late 1804
https://en.wikipedia.org/wiki/Sheheke

James Kipp was the agent at Fort Clark from 1822 to 1835. He spoke Mandan fluently and was married to a Mandan princess.   **https://www.legendsofamerica.com/james-kipp-fur-trader/**

Francis Chardon was the overseer of the Fort Clark Trading Post from 1834 to 1843. He had a long and colorful career with the American Fur Trading Company.
http://www.mman.us/chardonfrancis.htm

Prince Alexander Philipp Maximilian zu Wied-Neuwied (23 September 1782 – 3 February 1867) was a German explorer, ethnologist and naturalist who explored parts of Brazil and the United States. In 1833-34, he traveled

up the Missouri as far as Fort McKenzie in Montana. That winter was spent at Fort Clark. His journals accompanied by lithographs by Karl Bodmer provide a vivid picture of the Upper Missouri and its inhabitants.
https://en.wikipedia.org/wiki/Prince_Maximilian_of_ Wied-Neuwied

Karl Bodmer (11 February 1809 – 30 October 1893) was a Swiss French printmaker, lithographer, zinc engraver, draughtsman, painter, illustrator and hunter. He was hired by Prince Maximillian to visually record his journeys up the Missouri River in 1833-34.
https://en.wikipedia.org/wiki/Karl_Bodmer

An Indian Winter by Russell Freedman, Holiday House/New York, 1992, provides a fascinating look at the winter spent at Fort Clark by Prince Maximillian and Bodmer among the Mandan tribe. The book is full of accounts taken directly from Maximillian's journals and contains many drawings and paintings by Bodmer.

[i]
https://lewisandclarkjournals.unl.edu/item/lc.jrn.180 4-10-20#n07102002
[ii]
https://lewisandclarkjournals.unl.edu/item/lc.jrn.180 4-1805.winter.part1#n01

www.ingramcontent.com/pod-product-compliance
Lightning Source LLC
Chambersburg PA
CBHW061436160726
47995CB00003B/914